Praise for *Bracelet Honeymyrtle*

'Richly poetic and sensitive …
weight of its minutiae—a brill
a constant presentation of epiphanies …'
—Nigel Krauth, *Australian Book Review*

'This is a wise, mature book that will be loved as much as it
is admired.'
—Michael Sharkey, *The Weekend Review*

'… Judith Fox has carefully woven a delicate and restrained
tapestry of the human condition. She confirms a hunch that
many of us have: that fiction can be an open pathway
towards truth.'
—Ian Dixon, *The Press*

'This is an astonishing book …'
—Kate Veitch, *Sydney Morning Herald*

'Annie is a distinctive and memorable character, drawn with
tremendous empathy and insight, and her story … is an
enthralling and moving one.'
—Katharine England

'It's a long time since I have read a novel so touching and
uplifting.'
—Jo Riley, *Newcastle Herald*

'… an inspiring story of hope and goodness.'
—Bruce Morgan, *Tasmanian Metropolitan*

'Fox writes revealingly and with compassion …'
—Lyn Hughes, *The West Australian*

Judith Fox's first novel, *Bracelet Honeymyrtle*, was published to critical acclaim and shortlisted for both the Miles Franklin Literary Award and *The Australian/ Vogel Literary Award*.

Judith Fox has a BA in Communications from the University of Technology and a Master in Creative Arts from the University of Wollongong. She worked in the film industry, before becoming a publisher of academic texts. Born in Newcastle, she currently lives and writes in Sydney. Her second novel, *Scraping through Stone*, was published in 2002.

BRACELET
HONEYMYRTLE

JUDITH FOX

ALLEN&UNWIN

This edition published in 2002
First published in 1995

 This project has been assisted by the Commonwealth
Government through the Australia Council, its arts funding
and advisory body.

Allen & Unwin
83 Alexander Street
Crows Nest NSW 2065
Australia
Phone: (61 2) 8425 0100
Fax: (61 2) 9906 2218
Email: info@allenandunwin.com
Web: www.allenandunwin.com

National Library of Australia
Cataloguing-in-Publication entry:

Fox, Judith, 1959–.
   Bracelet honeymyrtle.

   ISBN 1 86508 868 4.

   1. Mother and child—Fiction. 2. Personal growth—
   Fiction. 3. Maturation (Psychology)—Fiction.
   4. Australia—Fiction. I. Title.

A823.3

Set in 10/13 pt Palatino by DOCUPRO, Canberra
Printed in Australia by McPherson's Printing Group

10 9 8 7 6 5 4 3 2 1

Acknowledgements

I would like to particularly thank Ron Pretty, of the School of Creative Arts, University of Wollongong, for his editorial advice and general guidance. I extend my thanks also to Tricia Dearborn for her considered readings of various drafts, to Bernadette Foley for her editorial lightness of touch and to Annette Barlow for her generous support. To my family and friends, my heartfelt thanks for the abiding belief in this book and the warm reception which greeted its arrival.

For Jyotsna

I rise with the sun. I place my slippers by the bed at night, alongside my dressing-gown draped over the bedroom chair. It is the delicate chair my father gave my mother in their first year of marriage. As a child I would slip into my parents' bedroom to sit on that chair. Our weights felt compatible. I would sit on that pretty chair and tell myself I was pretty too. I don't trust my weight on it now.

In the near darkness my hands and feet are sure as homing pigeons and I am slippered and gowned before I switch on the light. I sit at my dressing-table and plait my hair. Certain stretches are very difficult these days but this weaving of hair is a lifetime habit and it remains untouched by age. Deborah attends a gym and can do amazing contortions with her body. A bit like a circus act really. She put on a leotard and went through some routines for me once, for us, since I was holding Kimberley and we were the audience. Deborah had cleared a space in the middle of the living room and I perched myself in a corner, baby on my lap, both of us alert and attentive. Kimberley and I are not always so coordinated. Deborah put her body into positions I've only ever seen cats in. That thing that cats do, when they lean right back without support, stick a leg in the air then twist their heads around, all in the name of a good clean; well when cats do it, it looks graceful, but with Deborah it looked painful. The tendons in her neck were standing out and her breath was coming in sharp puffs. I was so taken aback I made some particularly asinine remark such as, Goodness aren't you a clever girl. No wonder she dislikes me at times.

I open my back door to sniff the cool air of early morning. Moisture clings to every surface. I put the jug on, juice celery and carrots, soften bran with milk and spread jam on toast. These days there's a big hullabaloo about natural foods and growing vegetables organically. It's all been done before. I've been drinking the juice of vegetables and eating what I grow, without the help of chemicals, all my life. But in eighty-four years you see a few turns of the globe. Eating the goodness provided by God went out of fashion in the Sixties, that time of hard shiny colours and materials. The food was like that too. Now everyone's jumping up and down about preservative-free food and compost in the garden. It was always waste not want not with us. As for all this talk about pesticides, there's nothing in a garden that a bit of urine here, a whiff of garlic there or a dousing with soapy water won't fix.

After breakfast I wash and dry the few dishes. Grey light is fingering the walls. I dust the bench free of crumbs, sweep the floor. I shower and dress then go outside to where a ramp leads to the yard. I replaced the stairs some years ago, for Bert's sake. The only way to get him outside was to build a ramp. He used to love to sit in the garden, a fine weave Panama protecting him from the sun, a rug handy in case he got cold. I gave him that hat. I liked buying good quality for Bert, it was one of my great pleasures. I'd wave to him from the bottom of the garden. He'd wave back.

I've inherited my father's green thumb. My earliest memory takes place in a garden. It is the orchard at Cecil Park, so I must have been less than five. There is a wild

2

profusion of blossom overhead, the sky is white with flowers. The trunks of the fruit trees are dark and knotted; I see faces and bodies in the hardened wood. My father, tall as a tree, takes me by the hand and leads me down the flowering avenue to the edge of the forest. Green paddocks sweep from our feet to a belt of trees in the distance, the blue sky pulses with hot light. My father sits me on a hummock of grass and kneels down by a dark hole in the ground. He reaches in and when he pulls his hand out his fingers are coated with black soil. The white of his fingers gleams through the blackness. He brings his hand to my nose and tells me to sniff. I do, and the rich, edible odour of moist earth fills my universe. 'This is good soil,' my father says to me. 'Never forget the sight and smell of good soil.' He then reaches into a hessian sack, lying damp on the ground, and pulls out a young tree. 'Watch me Annie,' he commands, and I do, compelled by the beauty of the soil and the little plant and by my father's passion. He settles the tree in the hole, and holding it with one hand, he scrapes back the earth with the other. He scrapes and shifts soil, lets go of the tree and tamps the earth with his palms. He looks at me, his eyes glad and bright and says, 'Come. Do as I do,' and I kneel eagerly by him and tamp and flatten, tamp and flatten. My hands are soon as coated as his. I am extraordinarily happy.

That first lesson in planting sent down a taproot and I've had the love of watching things grow ever since. Down the centre of my backyard lies a raised garden bed, full of vegetables to match the season. In the garage is a long bench where I pot plants, fiddle with handfuls of blood and bone and lime, mixing and sifting as if I were preparing a cake. Neat rows of garden implements hang from nails on a board above the bench. In a shed on the other side of the garden is the wheelbarrow and lawn-mower, and odd bits and pieces of furniture needing repair. Bert used to fix whatever was broken. He had a talent with wood. His broad thumb would stroke the grain and when he struck with metal it was never at the wrong angle or in the wrong place. There is furniture in the shed that's been needing attention for some time but I keep putting it off. A stranger's hands are not the same as Bert's.

I survey the garden. The vegetable bed needs turning, as does the compost probably. There's pruning to be done, stakes to be hammered in. I can't do any of this myself anymore, but there's a chap who mows my lawns for me, Ron, who'll take on the extra labour. He does a nice edge, does Ron, my garden's always neat as a pin when he's finished. I bend and pull a garlic bulb from the earth. Rich brown soil coats the papery skin. I could eat it there and then it is so fine. First light is warming from grey to rose as the sun climbs. From the pepper tree next-door a carol of birdsong vibrates the leaves. Everywhere freshness and good earth and the unmatched perfection of a new day. Music is welling inside me. I stand, full of song and silent, crowned by light, holding my sceptre of garlic. The neighbour's dog emerges from under bushes and lopes across the garden. He lifts his leg on the pumpkin vine. His curious long nose turns and I see him wink. At the incinerator he wheels and disappears down the driveway.

We had a dog when I was growing up. Roger the dog. He was always known to us by that appellation, it seemed to suit his generous personality. He was a grand pup, big-pawed and floppy-eared, patched in brown and black with an inquisitive eye. He was my brother James' dog really. When just a pup Roger the dog would sit on Dad's knee, ears at half-mast, those curious eyes bent on James who'd be some distance away trying to attract his attention. Dad would sit back, puffing on his pipe, enjoying himself immensely. One hand would lightly caress the dog's fur. Roger the dog would be visibly torn between the pleasure of that warm hand and warm knee and finding out what James was up to. Finally he would hurl himself off Dad's knee, all of him furiously concentrated on my brother. The two of them would race around the yard like mad things, wild with energy and excitement. Mum would come to the back door and stand behind the wire screen, silently watching. Dad would laugh, tip his chair back against the verandah wall. My brother was only nine then. A year later, when Roger the dog was killed on the road—the cost of his curiosity my mother pointed out—James was heartbroken. They'd been the best of friends. He never did get another dog. Mum said no.

I fetch a mat and trowel from the garage. Kneeling down I lift and turn the soil behind the garlic. I'll plant more cucumber I decide, a good sturdy vegetable. I go to rise but stiffness nails me to the path. I should have brought a stick. I try again but my knees cannot adjust the weight. Leaning forward I grasp a tomato stake and struggle to my feet. My breath is loud and uneven. I think of Kimberley, of her increasing weight. I hope I make the distance.

In the laundry I soap my hands and rinse them clean at the tub. I wash out my stockings from the previous day, using the yellow soap I've used all my life. If you've found something that works why swap it for the next shiny toy? A twist of rope is strung from one end of the laundry to the other, garlanded with rags and old towels and stockings. I take down the clean pair of stockings I washed out yesterday morning. I've been doing this in the mornings for seventy-odd years. I guess it's like the soap. It's not routine that pushes the life out of you, it's whether you pull it down on you like a lid.

My mother fled to Sydney when she was a mere slip of a girl, perhaps fearing the routine of tramping the Prospect Hills each Sunday, separated only by weeks of caring for poultry. Her father had been a schoolmaster, but bought a farmlet out at Cecil Park, at the turn of the century. He went in for poultry on his farm—being so used to hens as the family joke went.

As a young woman, each Sunday my mother and five of her sisters tramped the six miles of field that separated their farm from the meeting hall. There they held hands with other brethren and gave praise to the Lord. It was simplicity in faith they were looking for. The Church of England had gone the way of popery, all pomp and wardrobe and wrong doctrine. The other reformed churches were dead in spirit. Only the Bible and plain worship were true doctrine; God's word was there to be read if you stuck to the text. About ten years ago, when still a student, Deborah was babbling on about the text this and the text that. It took me ages to realise she was talking of novels and not the Bible. And there was me for a bit thinking she'd had a revelation of Spirit. I've never read a novel in my life but I could match Deborah word for word on how to read the text. Of course, as is usual with us, we'd be talking of completely different things even whilst imagining we were talking together.

So it was simplicity that counted. *Where two or three are gathered together in my name, there am I in the midst of them.* That's Matthew and he spoke for all good plain Christians with those words. All that was needed to worship were a few like-minded people wishing to praise the Lord, receive Him into their hearts, and follow His words. Hence my mother and most of my aunts hiking across the hills and paddocks to give thanks to the Lord. Elsie, Bertha, Eva, Muriel and Olive. And Clara, my mother.

I have a photo of my mother taken around this time, it is the earliest photo of her. It was taken in a studio not long after she was married, she is displaying her ring. She is beautiful, a fine-boned woman with a tiny waist, a heart-shaped face and a great mass of fair hair. She also has a slightly raised eyebrow, giving her a detached, ironical look. I can never be sure if this was in place before or only after her marriage. When I look at this photo I find it difficult to reconcile this wry beauty with my mother. The wryness had given way to something more like disapproval by the time I knew her. The mother I knew was a small, efficient woman, handsome but not beautiful, although the curve of her neck and the architecture of her bones should have made her so. She moved with decision and some quality of energy humming behind the capable gestures gave her movements the poetry of dance. Put like that I realise that my mother, for whom dancing was sinful, spent a lifetime dancing. And never knew it herself.

What was it like for my mother, to be so young and beautiful, traversing hill and vale each Sunday, the wind in her hair, the sun on her face, the grass alive with minuscule life; at the boundaries of properties groups of stolid cattle or those flirtatious horses which come right up to you, nuzzling your pockets for sugar; perhaps in the distance an inquisitive kangaroo, ears sharp and expressive paws holding some morsel ready while he watched these strange creatures with their muslin skins ballooning behind them when the wind caught them? Perhaps my mother dreamt of dancing, felt her heels lift with her skirts in the billowing wind, picked her way across the earth like a graceful brolga, locked eyes with the distant kangaroo and in that moment it was two wild creatures staring at one another, each liable to leap in the air at the slightest sound. But then she would have turned to see her companions, Elsie, Bertha, Eva, Muriel and Olive, placid cows ambling by her side. The dancing feet would have become aware of the sensible boots they were encased in, the wildness in her heart would have subsided, and perhaps at that moment she feared for her eternal salvation.

I always feared for my salvation, and so kept an anxious eye on God. It took Bert to get me to look to my own kind, to be a bit more down-to-earth about it. He was my saving grace that man. Literally. I was born Annie Seeds but I married Albert Grace. I had him for nineteen years, a mere breath in time. I was greedy for more, I felt like I just got started, having known long years of drought. You see those pictures in the newspaper when there's a big drought on, the emaciated sheep and cattle with their lips pulled back in death's smile, their felled bodies stiff on baked, cracked earth. They're black and white those photos. When I think of hell I think of something in black and white. As a child I had visions of fire and brimstone, a lively place compared to what I now see. I stare at those photos, those endless stretches of dead earth and dead animals and the recognition in me sears me like a brand.

There were those long years in black and white, and with Bert life came into colour. Then that terrible period when Bert was fading, eaten away in pain. I was glad to release him to God's care, to see him freed from suffering. Bert knew when to let go, knew when he was being called. Now Kimberley has come along, a gentle reminder that everything continues and I'm either in it or out of it.

There is the crank of metal in clean air. Mrs Johnson, whom I've promised lemons, at her clothesline. Outside a willy wagtail cocks his rudder at the sun. I scoop up half a dozen lemons from the basket on the floor; their fresh scent slices the laundry fug of soap and bleach. I bundle them in an old apron and carry them to the fence, just in front of the garage.

'Maggie,' I call.

My neighbour comes to the fence. She is spare and dark. 'Been doing a spot of gardening then?'

'Just pottering. I've some lemons for you.'

Maggie's face is set in lines of pain; I know she's not well. Her husband is aggrieved, doesn't like his comfort disturbed. They never had children because he was sure he wouldn't like it. Maggie has slowed over recent months and I've heard him shouting at her. I've been tempted at times to pick up a shovel and go in there and flatten him. Not a very Christian thought but gripping nonetheless.

'I'll make a lemon meringue,' Maggie decides. 'Col always likes a lemon meringue.'

I pass the lemons one by one over the fence. Maggie puts them in her clothes basket. 'The baby's not wearing you out now?'

'No. She's a blessing.' It's a reasonable answer. If I were twenty and felt as I do, I'd have to say the baby was wearing me out, but given my years I'm not doing too badly. I grasp the bony hand of my neighbour. A lemon bulges beneath our palms. 'I'm to see my doctor next Friday. Will you keep me company?'

My doctor is a homeopath and I've been trying to get Maggie to him for months. She's turning sallow and I don't like it. Mind you, that husband of hers'd be enough to turn any woman sallow. I know Dr Cooper would spot whatever's wrong with her. He spotted Bert's trouble before any of the other doctors. I'm not keen on other doctors, they hand out tablets like caramels at a Christmas party. I guess it's easier than thinking. The Queen uses a homeopath of course. I've always thought her a woman of great good sense.

Maggie's pulling her hand away from mine. 'He won't allow it.'

'It's a mid-morning appointment,' I say. 'You could do your shopping afterward.'

She hoists her basket on her hip. 'I'll think about it,' she says but I know she won't. The decision's already been taken. The dark shape of a man shows at the window. I lift my hand in greeting but am not acknowledged. Maggie tries to scurry.

It is still early. I take a duster from the bottom shelf of the linen press. In the living room I lift the ornaments one by one, wiping their curves and ridges before flicking the surfaces on which they stand. My favourite is the rectangular block made from paddle-pop sticks, some of which have been painted black. Depending on the angle it reads *love* or *Jesus*. I move it back and forth for the pleasure of the change. Whoever made it has a relationship with Christ that I understand. Sometimes you can see Him and sometimes you can't, but He is always there.

He is everywhere. This was so much a part of my childhood that I searched for God in the grassy runs between the fruit trees, looked under turnip crowns, opened wardrobes or peered under beds. When I was little I remember I approached my mother, to tell her that I'd not been able to find God, neither in the house nor in the garden. My mother washed my mouth out with soap for having blasphemed and told me to look out for my soul. I remember sitting under a fruit tree crying, with a terrible taste in my mouth. I was trying to find my soul and could not find that either.

I was often a disappointment to my mother. I was not the firstborn. My father followed my mother to Ashfield and they were married there. My mother came back to Cecil Park as Clara Seeds and moved into a two-room cottage, some four and a half miles from her parents' house. She was eighteen.

She made curtains, scrubbed the wooden table, became pregnant. My father built a sort of laundry out the back near the water tank. It was really just a lean-to, with moveable tubs and a copper. He chopped the wood for the copper and for the house, and upgraded his dray to a buggy to provide dignity for his wife when they sailed forth together. He bought her an enamel jug and sugar bowl, blue as a Sydney winter sky. He bought her the chair, its rush-bottomed seat delicate and pretty. They sat on the narrow verandah together, watching her belly swell. The child, my brother, they called William.

William was beloved. A beautiful, fair-haired lad, with blue eyes that didn't shy away from looking. He was dressed in immaculate white, with navy braid around square collars for a nautical look. His face, under the broad-brimmed straw, was transparent, perfect. A terrible drought hit the country and the trees and grass turned brown and burnt. The land was bleached of green. Water had still not been laid on and now had to be purchased, the tank being empty. They could run a stick over the corrugated ribs of the tank and the noise reverberated, shrill and hollow. That's a nasty sound for country folk. But still William was dressed in immaculate white. My mother fought the drought and its dusty shabbiness with all her might. My father could no longer grow corn or wheat greens for the poultry but William shone in fresh, pressed linen, sweet as morning glory.

My parents were both proud to thus spare their son. These family tales were relayed over and over, we grew up with their contours shaping our memories and with the knowledge of the struggle our parents had engaged in to provide us all with a life. They would tell us how the drought continued, how my father took to watering by hand, the pannikin spilling its precious contents onto thirsty soil. Dad still managed produce. It took nearly all day to drive to and back from Liverpool then, where the farm produce was sold to an agent for sale in Sydney. My father made that journey alone. Mum and William spent whole days together, with no one but themselves for company. I think of my mother, alone with her beloved son. In the midst of that clay-coloured expanse she could feast her eyes on her vision splendid, her very own creation. My arrival, four years into this bliss, must have come as an unwanted intrusion. I can't help but feel that the disapproval which marked my mother's bearing coincided with my birth.

Deborah did not change after Kimberley's birth, although it would not have been a bad thing if she had done so. She's too busy. My great-niece runs a market research company, whatever that is. Apparently it's all numbers and reports, statistical percentages, formulated questionnaires, tele-training and random surveys. I thought market research was seeing for yourself which greengrocer or butcher has the best produce for the best price but I've been told I'm hopelessly out of date.

Deborah doesn't make the adjustment from office to family life easily. I'm often feeding Kimberley when Deborah comes home. We'll hear the back door bang shut and Deborah's heels clicking across the slate tiles in the kitchen. She'll enter the room in a swirl of office couture and briefcase, bend to press little smacking kisses on the feeding baby. I'll feel a tremor pass through Kimberley's body and she'll pull faster on the teat. Every evening I wish for a quieter, less abrasive entrance but every evening when mother and daughter come together each is startled by the other's existence.

I don't understand Deborah's life, although I'm part of it. But then Deborah doesn't know the first thing about me or my life, she just thinks of me as some aged person she used to have to visit throughout her childhood; the Jesus freak (I've heard her say it to her husband Peter, she doesn't know I heard her), the giver of unwanted Bibles or the asker of unwanted questions, such as does she still go to church? To be fair, I've never handed out information about my life. I'm hard on Deborah, I know I am. She's very sweet under the shoulder pads. She was a sweet child too, smile like a Christmas tree, and a way of taking your hand at unexpected moments so that you felt silly with pleasure. We just grate on each other at times, which is to be expected in families.

Everything I am stems from and is shaped by my family. We were, are, Plymouth Brethren, although it is not strictly true to use the plural. I am Plymouth Brethren, but Deborah and Deborah's parents are Church of England. In fact, I'm not sure that Deborah is anything, although she's prepared to mouth something to keep my questions at bay.

I don't think Peter believes in anything, except economic theory. Certainly he makes a lot of money. So does Deborah. Their capacity to multiply dollars is, of course, one of the carriages liable to swing off the track when Deborah looks at me and thinks about my age. Because although the child care I provide is a free service they don't need it to be free. They like it to be free. There's more than enough money to pay someone but both Peter and Deborah like the idea of not having to pay. It's a balancing of options, my age versus their greed. It's a strong word to use about two people I'm fond of, but a true one.

I put down the Jesus puzzle and dust the pictures hanging above the sideboard. I pick up a small china cottage and inspect it. I don't know if it's my imagination but I'm sure there's more dust than there used to be. Maybe it's only the inexhaustibility of dust which wears me down these days. I used to believe I could combat it. Now I'm not so sure.

There was dust in the country of course, especially in spring when soil and vegetation began to stir after hibernation. We didn't stay in the country, although we all loved it. Not long after I turned five my father became ill. The doctor diagnosed typhoid and prescribed appropriately, but the medication did not work. That big strong man began to lose his strength. William and I were running through the orchard one day. William was only pretending to run so that I could keep up. He held out his hand to me and together we rounded a tree. Our father was kneeling, his head in his hands. At first I thought he was praying but then I saw that he was rocking back and forth. I could hear him making noises. William let go my hand and we stood there, in awful indecision. I heard William suck in his breath through his teeth and then he moved forward. 'Dad?' he enquired, as if Dad might startle and take to his heels. My father dropped his hands and struggled to his feet. He looked rumpled, not like Dad at all. He reached out and grabbed William's shoulder. 'Ah son,' he said. 'Son.'

I can't remember if the trees were in flower or bearing fruit, I can't remember if the sun was in or out. There was just

13

Dad's face, sunk in upon itself, and William's clenched neck. And me, looking on.

Dad put our house on the market and a Mr Lewis, of Morgan and Lewis, Estate Agents, Valuators and Auctioneers, came out from Parramatta to assess it. Mr Lewis was God's work revealed, Mum said. He looked like a thin, beak-nosed man with a balding head to me. He and Dad conferred together at the kitchen table and as a result we found ourselves living in a rented cottage at Parramatta. Dad now worked for Mr Lewis, keeping his books, noting down in his clear small hand the proceeds from sales and rents. Dad now also visited a different doctor, who advised that my father had never contracted typhoid. The medication had been all wrong and it was that which had made him ill. My father's health began to improve and he had a house built for us at Mays Hill, a mile or so from Parramatta. Dad looked after the sulky and horses for Mr Lewis and he drove them daily into work. I was glad to have horses by us once more. I liked their silken noses and the wash of their big lips as they fed from my hand. I liked seeing their big teeth, as big as my hand, which took the food but did not hurt me. I trusted them.

Bert was a bit like a horse, large and strong and dependable. He was a big man, bigger than me, and I'm no delicate blossom. He had big fleshy lips, good strong haunches and many's the time I've stroked his flank. I put the little cottage down quick smart and fan myself with my duster. Getting old doesn't change some things. Not at all. Here I am all hot and bothered and it's not the cleaning that's done it. I was no spring chicken when I married Bert; at sixty more like an old boiler. It is written that a woman's duty is to her husband and with all my heart I embraced my duty, only I wasn't too sure what it was. The night of our wedding I wore a nightgown in fine lawn which I had stitched for the occasion. The material was cool and soft against my breasts. A rush of longing and anxiety tumbled through me. I had no fear of

Bert's hurting me, only of my own unknowingness. I knelt by the bed, praying to the Lord for guidance. He gave it to me. At first I thought it was through the words of Peter: *For after this manner in old times the holy women also, who trusted in God, adorned themselves, being in subjection unto their own husbands, even as Sarah obeyed Abraham, calling him Lord, whose daughters ye are, as long as ye do well, and are not afraid with any amazement.* But when Bert entered the room and came to where I was kneeling, lifted me to my feet and held me against him I realised that the Lord had more in mind than the words of his apostle to guide me. That was a revelation now. Yes indeed.

Here I stand, twenty-four years later, cupping my breasts, aware that it's been a long time since anyone other held them. There's some would argue my taking care of Kimberley is the desire to be mother to a baby, even after all this time. Of course it's true in one sense. By the time Bert and I married there was no having babies, on my part certainly and possibly also on Bert's. I was Bert's second wife. His first wife Margaret had died of cancer some years before he met me. They'd been happy together but had never had children. In my time it was always the woman bore the responsibility when there were no children to mark a marriage. Harsh words, a barren wife. But look at Deborah. She wouldn't accept childlessness as her burden. She made them both take tests and lo and behold it was Peter's low sperm count that was causing the bother. There's no imagining Deborah sitting back and accepting that. More visits to the doctor, more injections and weekly tests followed. Kimberley wouldn't be here now if Deborah hadn't jogged Peter along. So I've no unkind thoughts for Margaret, although Bert told me that her family gave her a hard time. For myself I know the things that can be said of a woman. My unmarried state was commented on by all and sundry, from shopkeepers to cousins. I'm grateful to Margaret for having loved Bert so well for so long and I was angry for her when Bert told me of the comments she had to suffer.

I never knew Margaret in the flesh but I've come to know her in other ways. Through Bert, of course, whose loving nature speaks well for his first marriage, and through the bits of china and bric-a-brac he brought with him. When Bert was dying, also of cancer, I would talk to Margaret, let her know that I was caring well for him, as he had cared for her. I'd tell her she'd be meeting up with him soon, that they'd have lots of news to exchange. What with me and Mum, Bert had been busy. I was sure Margaret had been kept occupied as well.

Bert's niece asked me once if I didn't mind that he'd been married before. I said no, I was just glad he'd been loved. What was there to be jealous of? Joan pushed. 'But you weren't his first choice,' she said. 'Doesn't that rankle?' I clucked my tongue at her. 'How could it?' I said. 'We didn't even know each other then. It was Bert and Margaret who knew each other and she was his first choice. When it came time to know me I was his first choice.'

That Joan's a bit unpleasant. Likes to act nice, with a glossy smile and helpful hands. They'll be plunged in soapy water, doing the washing up and they'll hold up a cup here, a plate there. 'Royal Doulton,' Joan will say, as if surprised. 'That was my aunt's wasn't it?'

Generally, and I will admit to a great deal of satisfaction each time, I'm able to answer casually, 'No dear, that was my mother's.' She sniffs then, does Joan, and places the cup or plate in the dish rack with just a touch too much emphasis. And isn't she glad on those occasions when I tell her that the china she's holding did indeed belong to Margaret. 'Shame if it got broken,' she'll say, a pious look descending on her face.

'Well dear,' I respond, 'that's only likely if you keep holding it up with soapy fingers. The rubber gloves are there if you want to put them on.'

I can't help myself with that woman. She brings a sharp edge to my tongue. Whenever she visits me I can see how Margaret's family gave her a difficult time about being childless. The viper under the plump smile must be a genetic trait in that family, like red hair or blue eyes, the sort that skips a generation because Margaret was obviously free of it. Bert was always so patient with Joan. She never could get a rise out of him.

'Now Joanie,' he'd say, and her a woman all of fifty, 'now Joanie, come outside and I'll show you what I've done to the garden.'

Bert was a nurseryman by trade. To have someone close who knew plants, and loved them, was the greatest delight. All my life I've had a vegetable garden and some fruit trees, but Bert planted carnations and gerberas and asters, for colour he said, and he was right, they looked a picture when in bloom. We worked together in the garden, he and I, trading information, digging side by side, the sound of our trowels or spades in moist earth a companionable melody. He'd hammer in the stake, I'd rope the plant to it. I'd follow Bert as he mowed the lawn, gathering the clippings to strew on the vegetable beds and I'd think, I am your Ruth, whither goest thou there go I.

There's a knock at the back door. At least I'm not still holding my breasts. You can't be too careful after a certain age. Everyone watching you out of the corner of their eyes, waiting to catch the first glimpse of dementia. Old people are under suspicion the whole time. It's the opposite of those systems of justice where you're innocent until proven guilty. For us it's assumed we'll start dribbling or jabbering nonsense, when of course we're just tired and slow and our pesky limbs won't do our bidding as they ought. We'll be searching for a ten cent coin, and those small ones fall to the bottom of a purse, it's in their nature, and some well-meaning but mis-guided person will reach for that same purse and root around inside saying, now here we are, is that what you're looking for? All with a large blank smile, like you see on television, and no idea that the hapless soul before them is grinding her teeth in frustration, thinking get your fingers out of my purse. Instead we're supposed to smile sweetly and say thank you, for assistance which was neither required nor appreciated. The trick to helping someone is perceiving when there's genuine need. It's not that old people can't find their small change, it's that everyone else can't bear to wait while those old fingers fumble about their business. People should be thanking us for being kind enough to let them override their frustration at our expense.

Now there's a second knock. I haven't even got as far as putting the duster down. I get myself organised and go to the back door. Leaning against the bannister of the ramp, hands in pockets, is Ron. He's chewing at a corner of his lower lip, something he often does. It's a wonder he hasn't eaten himself away.

'Morning Mrs Grace,' he says as I unlatch the screen door. 'Nice one today.'

'Indeed it is. How's your family? Is everyone keeping well?'

'Can't complain. Fit as a fiddle meself but the missus feels the humidity.' He takes my elbow as we shuffle down the ramp. 'Reckon you could do with some stairs here. This ramp business is no good for you.'

'I know. It was such a to-do putting in the ramp though, that I put off changing it back.' Ron lets go my arm and we amble onto the grass. 'See that bed, could you give it a good turn? I'll add some blood and bone and we'll give it another turn later on.'

'Best be turning your compost too. You could use some of that.'

We pause and I rest my hand gratefully on the garden shed. 'I want to re-stake my cucumbers. They're sagging.'

'We had those tomatoes of yours in a salad last night. They were tasty all right—the wife commented.'

'They've been good this year. Nice to taste a real tomato after that pap in the shops.' I smile at him. 'I think it's the stuff we put in last year.'

Ron gives me a look of cameraderie. He's not a big one for smiling. This is about as close as he gets. The vegetable bed had lagged last summer and I decided to use night-soil to replenish it. Ron did not turn up his nose but helped me spread and mix. Once he'd commented that if his wife knew she'd die.

The sun has climbed and is in my eyes. I take my hand away from the shed where I've been propping myself. 'Come up to the house when you want a cup of tea. I'll get on with my cleaning.'

Back inside I sit down for a spell. I miss my little poppet but truth to tell I'm glad of a day off. Not just to catch up on household tasks but to catch my breath as well. The noise of the lawn-mower spreads through the house, familiar and comforting. I've always been partial to that sound, never found it an intrusion. Mum used to set her jaw whenever the grass was being cut, after petrol mowers came into use that is. Before that, William used to push the hand-mower up and down and scythe around the tree trunks. James took over after William married, until he couldn't manage it anymore. Poor James. He died of tuberculosis, at nineteen. I used to envy him until I met Bert. Thought he'd got out of it lightly, saw him fetching up at eternity ahead of everyone else as if that was something to be proud of. Now I think what a waste. What a terrible, terrible waste. The waste shocked me then too but I didn't dwell on it. It was redemption James and the everlasting life. Hallelujah. *Come unto me all ye that are heavy laden and I will give you rest.* I clutched that one, as if shedding a life was no more than putting your feet up at the end of a hard day's work. On his gravestone we put *Absent From The Body, Present With The Lord*, as if that were something to be grateful for. My choice, those words. I heard the clarion call each time I read them. Looking back I think someone should have put a sign on me that read *Present In The Body, Absent With The Lord.* Would even that have got through to me? I doubt it. James' death didn't. Not even that.

Pencil thin he was in those last months, his trousers baggy at the waist and his shoulders stooped. He'd grown a thin moustache, to give himself a dapper look. Instead, being so sunk in the face, it made him sinister, as if he were a villain. He died the year the Second World War started. In good health he would have signed up and who knows what would have happened to him then? At least he would have been with other young men, fairly bursting out of their uniforms with energy and vitality. Yet terrible things happened to those young men; the vitality got shot out of them, or bombed out of them, or seeped away in prison hutches. When I first saw the pictures of our men after they'd been released from Japanese prisoner of war camps the recognition jolted me. They looked just like James as he was dying. Hundreds of Jameses, grinning ludicrously out of their skeletal faces.

William was in the war. An officer, those fine features handsome and grave under his red trimmed cap. He had those piercing blue eyes, like our mother, and a splendid physique. By that time he was in his thirties, a man in his prime. He suited uniforms, he was the sort of soldier women used to go silly around. Perhaps it never occurred to him that not all women were silly. Mum certainly wasn't. I liked to think I wasn't, but I was. Present in the body etc. Beth, William's wife, was an exceptionally silly woman. Pretty, in that pink-skinned, fair-haired way, with beautiful clothes sewn for her by her sister. She laughed too much, was over eager with William and timid with Mum and me. After she had the children she grew fat. And had a nervous breakdown when William was away at the war. I never understood why William married Beth, but choose her he did, and the children at least were wonderful. Douglas and Audrey. Audrey is Deborah's mother.

The sound of the lawn-mower's coming from round the front now. The grandfather clock chimes, followed almost instantaneously by the one on the mantlepiece and the one in the kitchen. That big one is always fast by an instant. I've never been able to fit it to the others. I move off into the living room, pick up the duster and start work again.

It was at Mays Hill that I contracted scarlet fever. James was not long born so I must have been nine. There's not much I remember of the illness although at those rare times since when I have succumbed to a fever I recognise with horror the ruination of my tissue. It recalls something deeper and more rancid. I wake up in soaked sheets and cannot for a moment remember how old I am.

My mother told me that the doctor, under whose care my father's health had flourished, had told her to prepare for the worst. He did not think I would pull through. My mother's determination to reclaim me from the grip of fever was, however, unopposable. The doctor had warned that I had been weakened by the smallpox vaccination I had had the year before, which produced in me St Vitus Dance. My mother brooked no doubt. The fever was the work of Satan and I would be brought back to the fold of God.

Despite my mother's untiring care it was my father who was by my side when I awoke, the fever broken. I remember lifting my hand up to touch him and seeing how thin my hand looked. I wasn't sure if it was my hand until Dad took it in his. He whispered my mother's name and then, startling me, he bellowed, 'Clara. Come quick.'

He nestled my hand between his and smiled at me. He'd grown strong again, his moustache a stiff brush over his lip. He wasn't much given to touch or open displays of affection but he jiggled my hand and smiled and I lay exhausted against my pillow, happy to be with him. My skin was soiled

21

with old sweat but I felt free in my body, as if a weight had been lifted, a weight I had not even known pressed me down until it was gone. The curtains were drawn, the room dim. Sunlight poked through the centre parting of the curtains and lay like a narrow ribbon across the floor.

My mother came to the door carrying the baby. I can still see her small proud face. Her mouth took on a queer set and something gleamed on her cheek. Dad rose to his feet hastily, his heels knocking the chair sideways. He fished in a pocket for a handkerchief and stood by awkwardly, not touching Mum, but leaning into her. Mum took the handkerchief, gave James to Dad and patted her face. It was all over so quickly that I wasn't sure if I'd had time to blink, wasn't certain if those had been tears I'd seen blurring my mother's eyes. Dad still stood awkwardly by, but then he was unused to holding the baby and seemed caught off guard by the swaddled bundle he now held. Then my mother was bending over me, one cool hand touching my forehead, the other at my pulse. She lifted me to take some water. Her touch was brisk but gentle and her eyes kind. I bathed in that look, certain that I had pleased her. I vowed always to stay in good health.

As I convalesced I noticed I had trouble hearing what was said to me. I would wake to a yellow mess on the pillow next to my right ear. My mother was not pleased by this sign of continuing debility. She had prayed for exorcism. A partial result was not to her liking. As the days passed I gained slowly in strength but took to fearfully lifting my head from the pillow each morning to see if I had oozed. I always had.

Mum now lay a clean rag on my pillowcase each night. 'The good Lord let you live, Annie. If you are still troubled with your ear you must pray harder for your sins.'

'I can't always follow what people are saying.'

'You have stoppered your ears against the Lord. Look into your heart and see what wickedness lies there.'

I looked. 'I can't see anything.'

Mum gripped my shoulder. 'It was Eve who ate of the apple, Eve who had mankind banished from earthly paradise. Sin will always tempt you.' Mum's eyes bored into me. I could feel a sickly blackness pushing against my chest. 'The Lord marked you and then He spared you. Yet the Devil whispers in your ear still.'

Under Mum's hand I sank to the floor to kneel at her feet, my hands templed in prayer. 'I'm sorry, I'm so sorry. I pray and pray but my ear is still sick.'

Mum touched me gently on the head, a benediction. She sighed. 'You were sent to try me. You are my burden in this life but I love you with all my heart. Pray now to the Lord to cleanse your spirit.'

Each morning my knees felt the cold, stiff linoleum but my ear continued to weep its secret rotting message. Mum would take away my pillow rag for washing without a word. I was worried that my movements in sleep would dislodge the rag and I practised remaining quite still all night, my hands clasped on my breastbone.

After about a week Mum sat me down at the kitchen table. On it stood a bottle of olive oil, a tablespoon, a small bowl and a bottle of peroxide. A saucepan sat on the stove.

'I know the Lord intends you to be well. I've been guilty of the sin of pride, thinking my nursing had been enough to see you through.'

'It was, it was,' I said. I felt like crying. 'It's the darkness in me, Mum.'

Mum nodded. 'Yes, but more is required of me too. We will heal your ear together.'

She draped a tea towel around my neck. She picked up the spoon and went to the stove, and when she returned the hollow of the spoon was filled with tawny liquid. She tilted my head to the left and tipped the warm oil into my damaged ear. I felt it trickling through canals and seeking out passages.

It landed on the drum and I gasped with relief. Mum tipped my head again to let the oil run out into the bowl. Inside there was a loosening of moorings and a smelly substance was expelled with the oil.

Mum mopped my ear. 'That won't heal your ear but it eased the pain didn't it?' I nodded gratefully. Mum measured drops of peroxide into the spoon and tipped my head again. This time I felt nothing. Mum set me straight and said, 'This will dispel the darkness.'

Each morning, in the still kitchen, whilst the baby slept, Mum measured healing drops into my ear. Together we measured the days. These mornings were precious to me, my head wedged against Mum's breastbone, Mum's hands cupping my temples. I was no longer alone with my weakness. Perhaps God would now forgive me. Mum's care was intended to redeem me, surely He would be moved?

With time my ear did dry up. I still had trouble hearing but I grew adept at reading lips and I said nothing to Mum. She was working to redeem me. I prayed harder. Across our acre of land could be seen the houses of some of the children I had known through four years of school but I had no visitors. There was fear of infection still. I relied on William, who was now allowed into my room. He made hand puppets, from scraps of cloth Mum had decided were not useful for her sewing basket, and found objects. There was Bob, with a nose of tin and buttoned eyes, and Scallywag, all badly stitched corduroy and worsted. Scallywag blundered, dreadfully, but would always try again. Bob scolded and domineered. They were inseparable.

William was tall for his age, with a high brow and aquiline nose. Already grave and self-contained, one day he came home from school with a bloodied nose and went immediately to Mum to apologise for his stained shirt. He'd been obliged, he explained, to stop a bully terrorising some of the small children.

24

'I asked him to stop,' I heard him say, 'but he just jeered at me and even as I stood there he gave a little boy a Chinese burn. I asked him again to stop and he replied that he wasn't going to take any notice of a Bible-thumper. I pointed out that I could thump more than Bibles and punched him.'

I listened anxiously but Mum laughed. It didn't sound like Mum at all. Later William came into my room with Bob and Scallywag and started telling the story again. Bob was the bully. The puppets jostled and Bob's tin nose stuck out at a sharp angle as he sneered at Scallywag. I burst into tears. 'Stop it,' I cried, reaching out to still William's hands.

He let the puppets fall. 'Are you unwell?'

I hunched my shoulders and turned from him. 'No, but this isn't Scallywag's story. It's yours.'

'This could be Scallywag's story too.'

'No it can't.' My voice was shrill. 'Scallywag's not like you.' I wanted to hurt him. 'Go away.'

He left but returned the following day. I was guilty and miserable. I scuffed Scallywag. 'Silly. Say you're sorry.'

William smoothed a finger over Scallywag's uneven stitches. 'Now you sound just like Bob.'

As I grew stronger I hankered to join Dad and William in the garden. It had been a task shared by William and me to help Dad with the watering. We filled buckets and pannikins at the tap at the back of the laundry and emptied them over the loamy beds. This was before we had hoses. I had my favourites among the vegetables. I was fond of the spinach, which when strung by Dad seemed to defy gravity. I liked watching the tomatoes swell and ripen, the hard green balls turning flushed and soft. But my true favourites were the butter lettuces, perched on the dark soil like trimmings on a hat.

Dad washed out a wheelbarrow and lined it with a tartan rug. He arranged cushions for comfort and then he carefully laid me, still thin and fragile, in the homemade rickshaw.

William bowed deeply. 'At your service, Ma'am.'

He trundled me up and down the rows. Sometimes he passed me a pannikin, which I emptied slowly over the side of the wheelbarrow, watching the charcoal soil turn black. We didn't talk much. I liked being out there, watching the sky change at sunset, watching Dad's strong hands burrow into earth, pluck weeds from their secret roosts and gently fold back leaves in search of bugs or spots of mould. I liked to watch my brother, serious and private, as he filled and drained buckets.

One evening Mum walked down from the house to join us. James was fractious in her arms. Her white blouse gleamed in the twilight. I lay back against the cushions, a deep contentment seeping through me. I felt watered by God, gathered with my family under His gaze.

At tea that night Mum dished out potatoes, fresh from the garden, their new skins soft and golden in the lamplight. 'I don't think it's good for Annie to be outside at dusk. No more evening watering.'

Dad looked up from his knife and fork. 'I can't do it any other time.'

'Of course not. I meant no more evening watering for Annie.' Mum sliced open a potato and dabbed butter in the steaming split. 'Besides, it's too much work for William.'

'I don't mind. It's no trouble,' William said.

'That's a good Christian sentiment, but it's too much. It's taking you longer than normal and there's your homework after that.'

'I hadn't thought of that,' Dad said.

Mum patted his hand. 'You can't be held responsible to think of everything. That's why you have a helpmate.' They smiled at each other.

William looked to me. I was lying on the day bed, which had been brought into the kitchen for my convalescence. I had my tea on a tray. 'I don't mind the extra time. Would you miss it?' William asked me.

I felt like crying at the thought of being excluded from the evening ritual. There weren't words to explain how I felt.

'Annie, show us that you love your brother as much as he loves you.' Mum cut open another potato with firmness. 'You can help me prepare the vegetables. That way you'll still feel useful.' I could not avoid Mum's eye. I nodded assent. 'Good, that's settled then.'

Visitors started to call by, the children dressed in Sunday best, the mothers laden with sponges and lamingtons. It had been months since I'd spoken to anyone outside the family. With strangers I found their lips did not make sense. Mrs Stokes leant forward one day and touched me on the cheek. The three little Stokeses sat solemnly on their kitchen chairs facing me, their black boots dangling above the floor.

'Are you having difficulty with your hearing, dear?'

Mum was at the stove, making tea, but she turned quickly at these words. 'Of course she's not.'

Mrs Stokes stayed leaning forward, looking at me. 'I thought you seemed to be straining to hear, turning your head this way and that.'

Mum stood very straight. She turned her back on Mrs Stokes and lifted the kettle from the hob. 'Mrs Stokes is right Annie. It's very bad manners to be turning your head around as if it's on a swivel.'

'But if she is having trouble hearing, Clara.'

'She is not.'

Mrs Stokes clasped her hands in her lap and looked earnestly at Mum's back. 'But the fever. Many have found that it has affected the ears.'

Mum turned and with a smile put the teapot on the table. 'The fever ravaged my poor girl but when it left her it was as the Red Sea parting. Annie came safely through and the enemy of illness was destroyed in her wake.'

Mrs Stokes blinked and touched the cameo at her throat. 'Well,' she cleared her throat, 'that's very impressive Clara, but perhaps the tide caught her heels. A visit to the doctor would settle this.'

Mum smiled benignly upon her visitor. 'I can see that you have a neighbourly concern for us.' She transferred her gaze to me. 'Are you having trouble with your hearing Annie?' Held by the clear strong light of my mother's eyes I shook my head. 'Apologise to Mrs Stokes.'

'I'm sorry, for having swivelled my head like that.'

Mrs Stokes patted my arm. 'My dear, it was nothing.' She rose to her feet and the three little Stokeses rose with her, ducklings in a line. 'Thank you Clara, we shan't stay. We just dropped by to see Annie and I must be getting home to Jim.'

After Mum had closed the door behind our visitors she emptied the teapot down the sink. 'That woman has no decorum. Church of England of course.'

The next day Mum organised a visit to the doctor. On the appointed day Elsie came over to care for James and Dad drove us into Parramatta. Perched up high on the sulky I surveyed the streets and houses which were at once familiar and exotic. I felt like a visitor from a faraway land and noted each house, each clump of trees, dog nosing the gutter, child wheeling past on a scooter, with intense clarity, as if they were outlined in white light. We passed houses I knew and I studied them, searching for signs of change. They looked the same as when I had last seen them and yet different. I was exhilarated and frightened.

The appointment with the doctor was not until late in the morning so Mum left me with Dad while she went shopping. Dad sat me in a chair in an office which had a glass window through which I could see into another office. I was impressed with the heavy desk, the neat piles of papers, the full inkpots and stained blotter. I'd never been this close to business before. Through the glass I could watch my father in conversation with strangers. I was sure they were impressed too.

I sat very still, waiting. Mum always said that a body lacking quietness was a sign of impure thoughts. I often had itchings and stirrings in my arms and legs and I fought hard with them. Time slogged by. My body felt heavy, inert. It seemed to sink in on itself. I was at the centre of a huge cocoon, webbed and impenetrable. It pressed in upon me without weight. The flow of my blood was loud in my ears.

Mr Lewis opened the door. 'Great Scott! I didn't realise anyone was in here.'

Dad was right behind him. 'You remember my daughter Annie?'

'Of course. Of course.' He fiddled with his necktie and rocked back on his heels. 'Young Annie, yes. How's school going miss?'

'Annie has been unwell. It's been some months since she attended school.'

'Yes, yes, of course. You'll be back soon no doubt.' He turned to my father and relief visibly washed him. 'Walter, we need to discuss the Sutherland land. Could we . . . ?'

'Annie could wait outside.'

'No, no, if she's been unwell.' He sent me an erratic look. 'We'll step outside ourselves.'

I was wearing a navy pinafore with a starched white blouse. My box pleats had been ironed straight. Mum had tied my hair up in rags the night before and my ringlets curled around my cheeks. A perfect bow curved over my right ear. I studied the woollen cloth of my pinafore, losing myself in the minute warp and weft. Each thread seemed neither long nor unending but truncated and hairs-breadth in width. I was covered in tiny squares. I lowered myself further into the miniature world of the material stretched across my lap and began a game of noughts and crosses. I didn't know who my opponent was.

'Sit up straight Annie. You'll turn into a hunchback.' Mum was in the doorway, a few parcels in her arms, two spots on her cheeks hectic with colour. I struggled with tears that from nowhere blinked into view. I was safe and sound. Tears seemed out of place. Mum put down her parcels and looked at the little watch hanging from a gold bar pinned to her dress.

'I'll fetch your father. We can leave now for the doctor's.'

She left the room again and I surreptitiously wiped the corners of my eyes. When Mum returned she was accompanied by Mr Lewis, who heartily smiled at thin air and tucked his thumbs into his waistcoat pockets.

'Done a spot of shopping Mrs Seeds?' He rocked back on his heels slightly and then recovered himself. 'Young Annie's been quiet as a mouse. Why, she could have gone shopping with you.'

'My daughter has been seriously ill. She must not be tired.'

'Quite. Quite.'

'I'm glad to hear she was no trouble.'

'None at all.' Mr Lewis smiled largely again. It didn't seem directed at me or at my mother. 'Glad to have been of help.'

Dad came into the room and Mr Lewis, after the proper courtesies, hastily withdrew. He said I'd been no trouble but I knew it wasn't true. He was glad to be rid of me. Dad picked up Mum's parcels and I followed them to the stables, where the sulky stood ready. We rode through Parramatta until the river came into view. Outside a blank-faced building we stopped and Mum led me inside.

The doctor peered into my throat and prodded all around my ear. He held a candle high and stared down the tunnels of my ear, inspecting and investigating. He bent my head this way and that, he spoke to Mum about the stuff that had once oozed from me. They spoke of peroxide and then he whispered into my ear, close, so that I startled and coloured. He asked me the name of the King of England. He moved away and spoke again, this time asking me to name the date

Australia became a Federation. Another few steps back and I watched his lips anxiously. My address. Still further from me but his lips were visible. Again he asked for the name of the King of England. He nodded and adjusted his pince-nez. I was relieved to have got the test right. He said to keep up the peroxide treatment and that any lapses of hearing were simply due to the processes of healing. He asked my mother to bring me back in six months.

Returning home, my mother sat staring serenely at the passing landscape. From behind I could see the proud set of her shoulders and how she held her head high. I had a murmuring in my ear, not unlike the sound that swims up from a shell held close to the head. On the outskirts of town we passed Mrs Stokes, shepherding her young ones through a gate into a park. She saw us and waved. Mum nodded, her head still high. I waved to Mrs Stokes and turning, waved to the littlies who were jumping up and down, their tiny hands flapping the air. When I turned around there were Mum and Dad, sure and straight before me. The King of England was some make-believe figure, like someone out of a book, I thought, but Mum and Dad were special. I clasped my hands in my lap and set my head, stretching my neck to make it long. I wouldn't wave if I saw someone we knew. If people looked at us they would see I belonged. Look, they'd say, there go the King and Queen and Princess Annie. I nodded graciously at a cow, grass protruding from between its thick lips. Then I set my sights straight again as the carriage bowled us home.

I pull up outside the house. Women are clip-clopping along at a brisk pace, briefcases like port steering lights at their sides. The men move fast too, their heads down. It is not yet eight in the morning but there's no sleepy suburb feeling here. There are also no children.

Deborah opens the door for me. Peter has already disappeared, off down to Melbourne on an early flight. Kimberley's upstairs still, in her cot. My heart flies up the stairs, winging past the glossy bannister and groups of gold-framed prints on the wall. Poor little lamb, left alone to listen to her own breathing. However, I'm in no state to bring that cot downstairs so I clump around a bit in my sensible shoes and Deborah, who's fussing about in front of the hall mirror, gives a little start and says she'll run upstairs right away to fetch Kimberley. She's all in cream today is Deborah, like a sponge. I watch her as she goes up the stairs. No, not like a sponge, with its fluffed up texture, more like dough, smooth and creamy and dense.

There's the click of a key in the door and Marla enters. 'Hello Miss Grace,' she says, her generous smile making me feel it's been longer than a weekend since we last saw one another.

Marla comes in every morning to clean and wash. We have satisfying chats about what's best to use for carpet stains, or the relative merits of beeswax versus polish for wooden furniture. She's a very good, very thorough cleaner. She's also a Catholic, from the Philippines. At Christmas she gave me a plaster saint to put on the sideboard at home. I didn't have the heart to tell her that it meant no more to me than the image of a popular entertainer. That's what they are, the saints, the chorus of the Catholic cabaret. Yet Marla talks to them, takes them seriously. I've seen her on her knees in the kitchen, praying to one or other of them. And pray she must—her son's in gaol in the Philippines for unspecified acts.

'Deborah's upstairs, fetching down the cot,' I tell her.

'She need help,' says Marla, and trots off. 'Hello Deborah,' she calls and I go to put on the kettle. Even the fridge is a horror in this place. Normally fridges are homely objects; open them up and there's the comforting stage-lit interior, full of interesting bits and pieces. This one's light's so cold, bouncing off the silver steel, that it's a relief to close the door. There's hardly any chance to survey the contents.

Deborah taps into the room, still securing one pearl drop to an earlobe. 'Bye Aunty. Got to fly. Kimble's in the living room.'

'We need to talk about Kimberley's shots.'

Deborah is arrested, mid-exit. 'Her shots. It's in my diary but I haven't come to it yet.'

'Perhaps we could make an appointment now, to coincide with the date in your diary?'

Deborah makes a face at me. 'It wouldn't just pass me by you know.' I say nothing. 'I'll make an appointment this week.' She walks through the open doorway, then tips her head back and grins at me. 'I'll take her. You can come too if you like.' She gives me a mocking wave and disappears.

I don't like vaccinations. In my day they were frightful experiences. Not that they're fun now, but back then the needles were thick and the science imprecise. I was not the only child to become seriously ill following a vaccination. Deborah can go without me.

I carry the tea tray into the living room. Kimberley is asleep in her cot. I can hear Marla fiddling with the vacuum cleaner in the study. She's muttering imprecations, scolding the machine. She's always fidgeting with that vacuum cleaner. I call out to her and we sit down for our morning cup of tea.

'How you arthritis today?' Marla asks.

'Not bad. I'm quite limber this morning. Any news from home?'

On Sundays Marla talks to those of her family still in the Philippines. I dread to think what her phone bill costs each quarter. So far she's brought her mother out here, and she's trying to get her sister into the country. Her daughter came with her when she left. I've never been sure if there's a husband still alive, although I know her father's dead. Seemingly candid, there's a lot Marla does not reveal. I think her menfolk have caused her anguish more than once but it is not discussed.

'Fine, fine.' Marla takes a sip of tea and smiles reassuringly. 'Everyone fine.'

'Your sister—has she had any news?'

'Not yet. Waiting. She waiting.' I nod. I'm familiar with that. 'You go Church yesterday?'

'Yes, it was a good meeting.'

'Priest was good? Sermon was good?'

She meets my eye with an innocent look. This is an ongoing tussle. Marla knows full well that we have none of the trappings of what she knows as Church. Perhaps that saint for Christmas was not as innocent as it seemed. Underneath her toothy niceness is a mischievous spirit. I like her a lot.

'Only God was there to lead us, dear. Would you like another cup?'

She shakes her head and makes *brmm brmm* noises. We both peer into the cot. Kimberley is just beginning to stir.

'I'll take her outside,' I say. 'We'll sit in the garden for a bit.'

Marla gathers the tea things while I pat Kimberley's bottom for damp. From the study comes a fitful tune, building in strength and consistency. It's the theme song from *Oklahoma!* Marla has a rich voice, alto. I puzzle over *Oklahoma!* and then hear the vacuum cleaner. She's won the battle and is singing of wide open places.

I take Kimberley and her clean nappy out into the courtyard. Vines cover all the walls, with stone showing through here and there. The cover of neighbours' trees provides a dappled light. We sit on one of the cast iron chairs huddled round a table and look at the light, at each other. She is balling her fist, crumpling it into her mouth. She is still blinking awake. A sparrow wings down past the ivy and with a blur of feathers swoops vertically away. The garden is very quiet. There is the faint drone of the vacuum cleaner from inside the house.

I was at home sick for nine months when I had scarlet fever. I grew used to listening to the silence. After the fever broke there were long weeks of lying in bed, still too weak to lift a book or sew. Then more long weeks on the day bed in the kitchen and by that time my ear had stopped receiving messages from the world around me. Silence became ever more familiar. When I returned to school I had been away for so long that the teacher sat me with younger children, to repeat the rules of grammar and chant again the multiplication tables. I was large and obvious in that class. From across the hall I could hear what used to be my class singing during the music lessons.

At lunch I sat alone. The girls I had played with no longer knew me. It was as if we'd never chalked squares together on the grey asphalt, skipping from box to box under each other's critical eye. Dolly Clarke and Alice Waterhouse came up to me one day, when I was sitting on a bench near the boundary fence. They were holding hands. Alice's hair ribbon had slipped and dropped almost to her chin. My ribbon sat jauntily above my left ear, its bow as fresh as when Mum had shaped it that morning. My perfect bow did not console me. It used to be my hand that Dolly held.

'Are you better?' Dolly asked.

'Yes, thank you.'

'They said you almost died,' said Alice, her eyes lit with the talk of death.

'We thought you'd gone away,' Dolly said.

'I was at home. Getting better.'

I wished that Dolly had visited me. A letter had arrived from Mrs Clarke, requesting permission for a visit, and Mum had written back saying that the doctor had advised against it. I didn't remember him saying that but Mum knew best.

She'd burnt the letter from Mrs Clarke. 'It's better this way. You remember how upset you were after Mrs Stokes' visit. The Clarkes are Church of England too, and they seem to have no capacity for restfulness.'

I looked at Dolly, standing in front of me holding hands with Alice, and wished she wasn't a C of E. 'I'm fine now,' I said. Eagerness pushed up under my skin.

Dolly nodded. 'See you.' She tugged at Alice's hand and they waded back into the sea of bobbing pigtails, leaving me alone on the high-tide mark of my playground bench.

I cried at home that night. Mum wanted to know what was wrong. She said, 'God has a special purpose for us. You're crying for nothing. Remember the words of James: *Know ye not that friendship with the world is enmity with God?*' Still I sobbed. 'Annie,' Mum said, and held my head between her hands. When she held me I calmed. 'All you can think of is Dolly, but you're not thinking of Christ. John said to all Christians, *The world knoweth us not, because it knew Him not.*' Her tone grew mournful. 'Dolly is godless. That's why she's not your friend. You should be grateful. Now blow your nose, there's a good girl.'

At school Maisie now sought me out. Maisie had rolling eyes and protruding teeth. She dribbled on her sandwiches when she ate and laughed at nothing. When she sat next to me in the playground I hated her. She'd been seated with the littlies since she started school and had never progressed. I didn't want anything to do with her. Yet we were in the same class now and she sat next to me. I was making lots of mistakes in class. I couldn't hear the teacher when she was writing on the board with her back to us. I couldn't read her lips because I was at the back of the classroom. The teacher whacked me over the hand with a ruler for not trying.

I went to stand by Dolly and Alice when they were playing hopscotch at lunch time, hanging on the outskirts of their game. I hadn't been invited to play but I hoped perhaps I would be. Maisie approached.

'Annie,' she laughed. Her teeth were yellow. I could hardly bear to look at her. She rubbed her cheek against my shoulder. Dolly and Alice shuddered and walked away. I heard their voices, loud and disgusted.

'Phew. She smells.'

'Imagine talking to her.'

I turned to Maisie and yelled, 'Go away you stupid thing. Leave me alone.'

Maisie's eyes filled with tears. 'I thought you were my friend.'

Something vicious rose in me and I punched Maisie hard on the arm, in the muscle where it hurts. 'You don't have any friends. Don't you know that?'

Maisie just stood there, tears and snot running down her face. She licked at her face and I hit her again. 'You stupid thing. Why don't you blow your nose?'

She kept crying, her eyes rolling and her mouth open. I stamped my foot and then I found myself smoothing her hair back from her forehead.

'You are my burden Maisie,' I crooned. 'God sent you to try me.' I pulled my fresh handkerchief from my pocket and wiped away the tears and mucus. 'I will love you Maisie, because no one else will.'

Her tears ceased and she stood looking at me with such an intensity of longing that I wanted to hit her again. I knew I could. She would take it. I felt myself swell to double my size, my legs were strong as tree trunks; I was large and invincible.

'Go and have a drink of water,' I commanded, pointing to the bubbler. 'Then come back here.'

She loped off. I looked down at the ground, to where the chalked squares and stones of hopscotch lapped at my feet. With my toe I erased first one line, then another, then another. I kicked the stones away. The chalk was still lying by the marked-out game. I pocketed it. Maisie shambled back, water still dripping from her chin. I looked past her to where Dolly and Alice stood watching me. Not looking away I rubbed out another line. The air was hot and dry. My skin itched all over, as if I were wearing wool next to my body. I wanted to rub so hard that the ground would give way, opening up dark caverns reaching to China. I'd push Dolly and Alice into the hole. I rubbed and rubbed, the asphalt burning through the toe of my shoe. Alice and Dolly looked away.

'Maisie,' I said, and she waited expectantly, 'we will sit over there, under the trees.' She followed me to the bench.

'Sit,' I said, pointing. I sat down too and rested my hands in my lap. 'Now we will be very, very still.' Her limbs twitched but she remained seated. We stared out over the playground.

Kimberley is staring at a skink climbing the wall, its small grey trail the only movement in the still yard. She is fully awake. I smile at her and she blusters something back. I rearrange her in my lap to quell the throbbing that is building in my arms. It's a delaying tactic I know, as supporting her full weight is the problem, not her position. However, I can still hear the vacuum cleaner, a blowfly behind glass, so it's best if we stay outside.

'I'll sing to you,' I tell her and she acquiesces. I don't have much of a voice, but I can lift it in praise, so in a flagged courtyard in Paddington I warble,

Oh Blessed Hope, with this elate
Let not our hearts be desolate
But strong in faith, in patience wait
Until He comes.

At the sound of my voice the skink flees. Kimberley, rather more polite, simply turns her head away and dribbles a thread of saliva onto my arm. I fish out my handkerchief, tucked up my sleeve, and mop myself dry. Her face screws up with concentration and I feel the tiny body clench with the effort of passing a motion.

'I suppose patience is not something you cultivate at your age,' I comment as she clenches again. I remember my father telling me of an apocalyptically minded group called the Shining Lights, formed following a charismatic preacher's visit, out at Cecil Park. The group sat on a verandah in silence every Sunday morning for forty years, awaiting Christ's return. I've a soft spot for that group, having done my own forty-year stretch of silent time. I like to imagine that it was always a warm spring day and that they watched lambs gambolling in the sun. The reality must have been quite different. A verandah's no place to sit on a rainy day when the wind's blowing straight up from the Antarctic. Kimberley's right to turn from my song to more immediate concerns.

My ear is troubling me. Balancing Kimberley with one hand I dab at my ear with my handkerchief. The linen is spotted with smelly effluent when I finish, the same smelly effluent I've been contending with since I was nine-years old. The only time the ear has not wept its sad tale was when peroxide was being administered daily. The peroxide, of course, damaged the ear irrevocably. Some days are worse than others—I'm never sure why.

The ear was dry when Mum took me back to the doctor. Again he peered down the funnel of my ear and poked around the side of my head. At the end of the examination he sat down and cleared his throat.

'It all looks much the same. How's your hearing?'

'It's fine,' answered my mother. I sagged with relief. I hadn't known what I was going to say.

'Would you like me to test it?'

Mum looked at me. I felt sick at what she would say were she to discover the blackness still lodged in me. She turned back to the doctor. 'Not if you feel it is the same as before. Shall we continue the treatment?'

'Yes, keep the peroxide going. It's clearing the problem nicely. Small daily doses should be the end of it.'

But in six months we were back at the doctor's. Mum grew irritated with my lack of response or understanding when she spoke to me at times. One day she covered my good ear, having stuffed a rag into it, and whispered into my bad ear. Of course I had no idea what she was saying.

She removed the rag, her face taut. She slapped me across the cheek, hard. 'You lied to me. Your own mother.' I stared at my feet, trying not to cry. 'Look at me,' she directed and when I did, forcing my head up, I saw disgust written plain on her face. 'You are a miserable girl. What are you?'

'A miserable girl,' I repeated miserably.

She slapped me again and I began to whimper. 'Go to your room.'

At tea Mum was lit with righteousness, as at a meeting. After prayers she announced, 'This family tries to bring Christ into our lives every day, but we have a liar in our midst.'

Disturbance rippled round the table. 'What has happened?' Dad asked.

Mum looked at me. 'Annie has for months been telling us that her ear is getting better. Today I found out that she's lost the power of hearing in her ear.'

The words reverberated in my good ear. I had put my hearing on my pillow one night and when I had woken it was gone. Lost.

'But this is terrible,' said Dad.

'Evidently.'

'The doctor tested her hearing,' Dad said.

'Annie read his lips. Am I right?' She was looking at me.

I nodded. I was increasingly damp skinned. My skirt clung to my chair. Dad looked awful.

'Why didn't you tell us?' he asked me.

I couldn't remember why. It had seemed clear at the time. Yet I'd lost my hearing and kept it secret. Wilfully. I didn't know why I'd done that.

'Answer your father.'

'I hoped it would come back,' I improvised. My voice was scratchy. A poor, thin voice.

Dad got up from the table. 'I can't tell you how disappointed I am in you. No tea for me thanks Clara. I'm going outside.'

William cleared his throat. 'Annie's been practising her hearing. I've seen her, practising to get it back.'

'Stop trying to protect your sister. She knows she's done something wrong.'

The baby began to cry, a wailing that spiralled and spiralled and spiralled. Mum stood to pick James up and cradling him said, 'William, you may leave the table.'

'I haven't finished my tea.'

'I said you may leave the table.'

William lay down his cutlery. I was by now glued to my chair. He lifted his finger to the bridge of his nose, watching me intently, and with a sharp turn of his wrist he lowered his hand.

'What was that?' Mum asked.

'A salute,' William replied.

'You salute a liar and a cheat? Is that who you think should be saluted?'

'I saluted her because she's Annie.'

'What does that mean? You salute your King. You salute your commanding officer. You salute those for whom you have respect.' She shifted the baby, whose cries still punctuated the air. 'You are dismissed from this table. I want you to think about respect.'

William nodded stiffly and left the room. Mum came to stand over me. 'I want you to look at what you've done. This family has gone without its tea because of you. Your father's outside, suffering, trying to understand why you've turned out this way when he's given you a Christian start in life. And your baby brother,' here she held the baby out to me, an exhibit, 'look at him, his pure innocence threatened.' I couldn't even cry. I sat dumb. 'I am at a loss to understand how you could lie to me.'

I was sick. Obviously very sick. I didn't know how or when it had happened. I wanted to die.

'Clear this table and then we will pray.' Mum leant down until her face was inches from mine. I started to shake. 'Pray and pray. We will pray for your life.'

How I prayed. I asked God to cleanse me of my sins. I tried to make myself open, to reveal everything to Him as if I were the desert or the sea, but I remained hilly and forested, with dark caves hiding from His sight, covered over so that no light penetrated. I was a secretive girl. My mother kept reminding me of it.

'My daughter is secretive I'm afraid,' she said to the doctor upon our return visit.

'It has cost you your hearing Miss,' he said to me. He took a large syringe and inserted it into my ear. 'I'll take a sample Mrs Seeds and we'll see if anything's salvageable.'

There was pain. Mum looked on calmly while I squirmed. I bit my tongue hard to distract myself. 'Something's still alive,' commented the doctor with satisfaction. 'A good sign. Definitely a good sign.' He fiddled with the syringe and other instruments, not meeting either of our eyes. 'Now as for the peroxide, I'd stop that.'

'Why?' asked Mum.

The doctor still wouldn't look directly at us. 'It clears up the mess all right, but I think at this stage we need to see what's there, mess and all.'

Mum didn't miss a beat. 'If my daughter had been honest with us Doctor, we'd have been investigating without perox- ide earlier.'

'That's right,' said the doctor, able now to meet our eyes. 'That's right.'

My family adjusted to my having carelessly lost my hearing. Everyone made an effort to speak to me on my good side. My mother wrote a note to my teacher to let her know of my special problem. She also questioned me more closely on everything I did or said, suspicious of my intentions. My father seemed to have his disappointment welded to him like a shield. He no longer showed me special tricks with planting or fertilising as once he had. When I accompanied him in the garden or to care for the horses he was matter-of-fact, business-like. I no longer felt that we shared something particular. I had broken that link as well.

At school I remained concerned with Maisie but less so than before. She followed me around, would sit beside me on the bench at recess whilst I sat, hands clasped, eyes ahead, communing with the Lord. When I bothered to look at her, her face was furrowed with anxiety. Her hands groped at me one day.

'What's wrong?' she cried. 'Why don't you like me anymore?'

I patted her. 'There, there. Of course I like you Maisie. I'm busy.'

'Doing what? What are you doing? You just sit there.' She was dribbling and her mouth was loose.

'I'm talking to God. It's very important, more important than you understand.'

'Let me talk to him too.'

'You need to be very good to talk to God.'

'I'll be good.' Little flecks of spit caught on her chin. 'What do you want me to do?'

'There is nothing you can do,' I said sadly, shaking my head. 'Nothing. You're either good or you're not.'

Her face fell in upon itself. Her hands were grabbing at me. 'Show me. Show me.'

I was big and strong. 'I can't. Poor Maisie. You're just not good enough.' I rose to my feet, calmness radiating from me like light.

'Don't go,' wailed Maisie. 'Stay here.'

'I'm busy,' I said. As I walked away I heard her howl, high-pitched and shocking. Years later, when Roger the dog was run over outside our front gate, the first we knew was the sound he made. I recognised it. It was the sound Maisie made as I walked away from her.

After changing Kimberley's nappy I warm a bottle. She feeds slowly, almost languorously. It is past midday by the time I put her down. The living room is cool and shadowed. I prepare a salad for lunch, a large one, as Marla is always hungry after cleaning. There's something very satisfying about the physical exertion of cleaning, the manual labour involved in ordering a household. I miss being able to push myself in that way.

'Marla,' I ask over lunch, 'where does your name come from?'

'Holy relic,' is the prompt reply.

I must look sceptical because Marla smiles hugely. 'No can fool you Miss Grace. My mother named me after heroine in book, her favourite book.'

'A novel?'

'Yes. Marla was American girl in love with Filipino boy.'

Names are funny things. They count for more than people imagine. My mother named me after the woman who had been her guide to church on the day of her wedding. Did my mother dream of freedom when she chose my name, did she intend to bestow on me the gift of flight? Marla's mother obviously dreamt of romance. I cannot believe my mother named me to celebrate a time of happiness. In my bones, these old creaking bones, I feel she named me as a punishment, to remind herself of the perils of desire. I do not believe the story that my mother named me after Annie Vale because she was a dear friend. If she was such a dear friend why did she and my mother never correspond or visit?

I clear the lunch dishes and absent myself when the small dark woman arrives to arrange the flowers. She has a name I can never remember. It bespeaks a lack of kindness and neighbourliness on my part but I cannot seem to do otherwise. I know in some way she has been damaged by the war, the second one, but the effort to reach her is beyond me. I had far more energy thirty years ago when I tried to convert the Muslim greengrocer in the main street at Penshurst.

The first war was the one that scarred my family, although I was too young at the time to understand what was happening. Two aunts lost husbands, others lost brothers-in-law. Due to his medical history Dad did not sign up. William was only a lad and it wasn't until well after the cessation of hostilities that he was able to join the Voluntary Corps. James was not even born when the war ended. He came with the new decade when everything seemed hopeful still. James was a lovely lad, very lively, with a clowning spirit. He could make us all laugh. It became my job to escort him to school. We'd set out early so that he could talk to all the horses on the way and watch the ants busy at work at the corner of the Forresters' land.

'Why are you always in trouble?' he asked me one day, as he was poking in the dirt with a stick.

'I am not always in trouble.'

'You are too. Mum's always angry with you.'

I sucked air through my teeth noisily. 'Sometimes I'm very wicked. Only I don't mean to be.'

James, still squatting, contemplated me. 'Isn't the Devil wicked?'

'Yes.'

'But you're not at all like the Devil, so how come you're always getting into trouble?'

'I've just answered that.'

'No you haven't.'

I yanked him to his feet in exasperation. 'You'll get dirty playing down there. Come on.' I dusted him while he stood, patient, staring out into the distance.

'I'm not dirty you know,' he said. I stopped flapping my hands at him. I felt like I was going to cry, so I set off down the road.

'We'll be late,' I called.

He ran to join me and slipped his hand into mine. 'I don't think it's fair that you're always getting into trouble.' I squeezed his hand and sniffed back the tears. 'You're hurting me,' he said and I let go his hand immediately. I felt my awkwardness like a handicap.

'Look at the ants,' James marvelled and dropped again to his haunches. I dropped down with him, careless that my hem was trailing in the dirt. The ants, big bull ants and hundreds of little black minions, were busy funnelling and fetching. We watched two small ants struggle with a gumnut, ten times their size. They heaved and strained to no avail. Other ants joined them and the slow tussle resumed.

'They're something aren't they?' I said. James pushed his finger into the dirt and made a small barricade, to see what a line of ants would do. They made their way around it.

At home I was now accomplished in sewing, cooking and cleaning. When I helped Mum with the baking I was happy, although not being as fast on my feet as her I had a tendency to get in her way. The kitchen would be humming with the energy required for cakes and biscuits and bread: the fast whisk for eggs, the heavy beating for flour, eggs and sugar, the slow folding in of egg whites and the kneading that works you hard in the shoulders. Bread would be rising in corners, tea towels over the bowls, and the air was redolent with yeast and spice. I loved how we started with the ingredients all lined up on the table as separate items and ended up with trays of golden delight. I was no good at chemistry at school but I understood intuitively in the kitchen about the consequences of heat on matter. The menfolk would wander through, appreciatively sniffing the air or surreptitiously lifting a hot biscuit from the tray. We'd turn around to discover empty corners, hemmed in by rows of Anzacs or macaroons or melting moments. I always gave James the bowl to lick, he had a gift for sauntering through the kitchen at precisely the right instant. He'd sit on the kitchen stool, the bowl on the table in front of him, running a finger inelegantly around the inside, his satisfied mouth outlined in cake mixture.

I loved to cook. I loved the pleasure of providing for others, of taking the produce of the Lord and shaping it to a meal. Mind you, there's a lot of the Lord's produce that doesn't like being tampered with. Put spinach in a pot and you've reduced a fine flavoursome vegetable to something poor and weak. It's true of most vegetables: they're better raw. But take an egg, a chicken, a rasher of bacon and some breadcrumbs, put them together and apply heat and you've something the hen never imagined she was capable of. My chicken pie and date loaf were my specialities. They never let me down.

I wasn't such a good dressmaker. My stitching was small and even and I finished well but I had no skill in cutting.

'Think about what you're doing,' Mum remonstrated, as I nosed the scissors through the material.

'I'm trying, but they won't go the way I want them to.'

'You've got control of the scissors; make them do what you want.'

I would apply myself with renewed fervour to the task but the scissors remained obstinate to my direction. Mum would wander back into the dining room where material and pins were spread across the table and shake her head.

'You have no ability to shape things.'

I was downcast but in fact there were things I could shape, although certainly not dresses. For James I would mould gingerbread men, without aid of a cutter, with sultanas for eyes and slivers of almonds for the mouth. I loved to order the pantry and the linen press. It became a weekly passion to run my hands over the shelves, straightening jars or piles of pillow cases, checking for mouse droppings or moth holes. Of course, Mum's pantry and linen press were already in good order, I was simply maintaining them, but each week I would be dissatisfied until I had stroked a straight tower of linen with my fingertips, feeling how each fold sat neatly upon the one below, nothing out of line, or had set the canisters in neat soldierly rows, so that the line of sight was dead straight.

Three times a week William chopped wood. I was responsible for the kindling. I was rather in awe of him these days, he was so much of the grown-up world of work and army life having joined the Voluntary Corps as soon as he left school and took up his apprenticeship. He was as sweet to me as ever, would tell me stories of the military camps he attended, would describe all the different lads he met, how much they varied one from the other. He'd been responsible for making his bed since an early age so it hadn't come as a shock to have to square off his camp stretcher. Apparently some of the others were big babies, and the sheets and blankets crumpled in their hands, usually at the most inopportune moments, such as before an inspection. From the workshop where he was apprenticed came more stories, tales of men and their habits. I thought they sounded rather ungodly, some of them, but William had time for everybody.

It wasn't like that at home. We knew all the families who attended the meeting but we were not a visiting family, and Mum was none too keen on being visited. As she said, although the brethren were our folk, they were not family. At assembly there were mutterings of discontent, for another group wished to use the hall for worship, but they were of a wrong doctrine. The elders had spoken of this matter but the apprehension belonged to the whole body of believers. We did not own the hall, we only rented it, so it was not within the power of the assembly to refuse this other group. The landlord did not belong to either group. Dad had found the hall through his work at Lewis and Co. and there were those who expected him to be able to influence the outcome. He had represented our views to the landlord but had received an unsatisfactory reply.

The evening before the meeting, when Dad was to advise that the landlord had not changed his mind about letting this other group use the hall, there was a massive storm. Huge bruised clouds clumped together until the sky hung like a dark wave over our heads. At four in the afternoon we needed to light lamps inside the house being afraid to turn on the electric lights. An ominous stillness descended, broken only by the desperate calls of birds settling flocks in trees. The air threatened, as if about to punch. Missiles of purple lightning hurtled through the blackened sky, their power startling the landscape which lay unprepared and unprotected.

I was standing in the front parlour with William and James watching through the windows. The dark skirting boards and picture rails and the crimson stuff of the chaise-longue absorbed what little light there was. We had not lit the lamps in this room and the menace of the approaching storm had me trembling, a blancmange in a dress. William was very quiet, although at the first deafening explosion of thunder he cried, 'Oh it's grand!' James was torn between exhilaration and terror. He held fast to my hand, hopping up and down as if he wanted to go to the toilet. When the second roar of thunder cracked above our heads he burst into tears. William seemed to shake into himself and he took James' other hand. 'Hold on little chap. It can't hurt us in here.' I squeezed James' hand hard on the other side. I wasn't as sanguine as William.

To return to the kitchen from that darkened auditorium

was an enormous relief, at least for James and me. The kitchen was a golden capsule into which we neatly fitted. There was tea and toast and we sat together while rain fell like fists on the house and the wind shook windows and made us worry for the chimney. Beyond the glass it was quite dark. We spoke of the great flood.

Which turned out to be very apt, for when we arrived at the meeting hall the next morning we found the structure flattened, its logs scattered over the paddock in giant disorder, its roof a kite long since disappeared over the trees. The entrance stairs stood firm, an ungainly stump of carpentry. The assembly did not wander very far from the ruined building, although people were pointing remains out to one another. James was dodging through the group, in a state of amazement. He would run to us, a chair leg grasped in his hand, or a shard of smashed lamp. 'Look, look,' he offered, then he was off again. From behind us a man's voice called out, *The fountains also of the deep and the windows of heaven were stopped, and the rain from heaven was restrained.* A murmur of approval swarmed into the air. The same voice cried, *And the Lord said, Behold the people is one and they have all one language; and this they begin to do: and now nothing will be restrained from them, which they have imagined to do.*

It had now been spoken of. We had wanted to keep the false believers out and God had heard our prayers. The assembly knelt, the moist earth sinking to the shapes of knees. We gave thanks to the Lord. We knew ourselves to be receivers of grace. In His excellency He had overthrown those who had risen against Him. He had sent forth His wrath, which had consumed them as stubble. We who had listened and obeyed, who had kept His covenant; we had been chosen, we were a peculiar treasure to Him above all others. William whispered in my ear, 'We also have no place to worship.' I gave him a pitying look. He had completely missed the point.

I seem to be missing the point here. Marla is telling me a

long involved story about her family. There's an adulterous liaison, I think, and she tells me the wife has been in hospital for a long time as if that's a justification. I haven't worked out what's wrong with her yet. There was a pregnancy, the mistress I think, but she miscarried. I have to admit I'm very confused. I didn't know any of Marla's relations ran a fancy restaurant. She has not mentioned it before. Marla, who sees marriage as a sacred contract, nonetheless seems partial to the adulterers. True love, she's commented more than once. Then she says something about the husband really seeing his wife in his mistress, as she was before the wasting disease, because they both have long blond hair. My comprehension comes to a standstill.

'Did they dye their hair?' I ask.

Marla looks pained. 'No. Beautiful gold hair. Natural.'

'Everyone in your family has black hair surely?'

'Yes.'

'How did these two women come to have blond hair?' I'm fiddling with my hearing aid in case I have it set too low and am missing some vital clue.

Marla is exasperated. 'Is TV. No my family. You no listening, Miss Grace,' she accuses.

'I am listening,' I answer firmly. 'I simply don't understand.'

She clicks her tongue at me. 'You no watch soap opera?' I shake my head. I think we're veering into plaster saint territory here. 'I do,' she says proudly. 'I tape each day and watch at night.' One of those bland expressions settles on her face. She's hatching mischief. 'You could borrow tapes. I lend to you.' Her tone is unctuous.

'No thank you my dear.'

'Lovely love story. You like that?'

'I had my own lovely love story.'

Marla is serious again. 'You very lucky. I no have a love story.'

I take the plunge. 'Where is your husband?'

'Here, in Sydney. He no work but. He gamble, he drink. Like father, like son.'

The bitterness and resignation in her voice is awful. I point to the cot. 'There's our love story. She's much better than TV.'

Marla smiles. 'This baby lucky to have you. This baby grow up in your heart.' She leans over the cot and makes little cooing noises. 'Love baby. Precious baby.' She straightens up. 'Time to go. Back to husband, back to mother.'

'We'll see you tomorrow.'

'Tomorrow I come back to baby hope.'

Marla is soft and plump, a well-fed pigeon. She puts her shoes back on and I notice that her feet are swollen. Her face doesn't show it but I imagine that it must hurt to squeeze the flesh into the leather. I suggest parsley tea and cucumber to reduce the swelling. They help push out the fluid.

The house smells sweet and fresh. There's a truly absurd centrepiece of flowers in the living room this week. The stems stand feet tall and the arcs of pussy willow which act as the sustaining backdrop make circling the coffee table a hazard. It wouldn't be out of place in a concert hall. It's out of place here.

I follow the afternoon sun and decide that if the good Lord in His wisdom had wanted me to be a cat I wouldn't have minded at all. I wanted a cat when I was a little girl but my mother said they were strange animals, well known to be the Devil's familiars. Small furry bodies padding across my path frightened me greatly after that. A cat had only to look at me and I became convinced that the Devil was seeking to enter my soul. I lost all appreciation of their grace and beauty and it wasn't until Bert entered my life that cats assumed a different meaning for me. He was fond of them, had been used to living with them as Margaret always kept a cat. They're clever animals. A neighbouring cat sensed that Bert was amenable and took to visiting us. Bert would point out with approval how the big ginger fellow followed the sun, always positioning himself for the best degree of comfort. He was an old cat and he died before Bert. Bert missed him. I suggested getting a cat to please him but he said no, if there's one around looking for company it'll find us. But no more cats turned up.

When Deborah arrives home Kimberley and I are at the end of a bottle feed. She's tired but content. I'm just tired.

'Hello babycakes,' says Deborah, lifting Kimberley into her arms and then promptly returning her to mine. She pours herself a drink. 'Don't the flowers look great this week?' I busy myself with Kimberley's bib and treat the question as rhetorical. 'Did you two have a good day? I had a great day, signed up a new client.' She rubs her fingers together, the gesture of usury. 'Big big bucks. It'll help keep the wolf from the door.'

'I hadn't noticed him prowling around outside.'

'You can never be too careful. Rainy days and all that.' She sits down and motions to Kimberley with her glass. 'There's this one's education to think of. What if she wants to go to Harvard Law School?' Her eyes narrow and I can see her speculating. 'That'd be something, wouldn't it? International law'd be the thing to go for. That's a global career. The other possibility I've considered is the media; her own current affairs programme.' Deborah clicks her fingers. 'Of course, she could combine both. What a coup. She'd be good at that.'

'She's good at soiling her nappies,' I comment. 'For the most part she's good at taking her bottle.' I smile at Kimberley.

'You've got to think ahead Aunty. The girl's got to be somebody.'

'She is somebody. She's Kimberley, your daughter.'

Deborah downs the rest of her drink. 'She doesn't want to just be her mother's daughter. I mean, you were. What good did it do you?'

There's a mean edge to the question but I don't think she's aware of it. 'It made me who I am,' I reply quietly.

Deborah dismisses this. 'That's all very well when you're little. I'm talking about what happens when you're a woman.'

'So am I.'

'Aunty, you never worked. How you feel about yourself, how you are perceived, is inextricably linked with work, the capability to do it, the recognition that comes from doing it. In your day it was perfectly acceptable for women not to work but that doesn't apply any more.'

'How you feel about yourself is a lifelong task between you and God. I would hope you would feel the same about yourself if you lost your company tomorrow and went out cleaning.'

Deborah is clearly offended. 'I would never clean for a living.'

'That makes you foolish, not clever. What's wrong with cleaning?'

'Women have done the cleaning forever. It would be some huge regressive step to do something like that.'

'Where does Marla fit in then?' We are glaring at one another now, two cats bristling with hostility. She thinks I'm naive, I think she's deluded.

'Marla likes to clean.'

'Marla might like to be an executive. Unlike you she doesn't have the choice.'

'Of course she does. It's an open labour market.'

Quite suddenly I feel very old and glum. 'That's Peter talking, not you.'

Deborah stands, restless energy fading. She has the grace to look ashamed. 'Aunty, I don't know what it is, but you make me so mad sometimes. I feel I could hit you.'

I shift Kimberley's weight to the other arm. 'Sometimes I could hit you too.'

She grins at me, a seven-year-old larrikin. 'That'd be a sight wouldn't it?' She runs a hand though her hair and the perfect statuary gives way to something softer. 'I never argue like this with Mum. She sort of disappears if I start pushing.'

'I didn't argue with my mother either.' My hands around Kimberley are knotted, sepia coloured. She is God's work made manifest. I think, here we are. Wonder is beating in my blood.

'I don't believe you,' says Deborah. She comes over. 'Can I take her?' Kimberley is burbling into sleep, small sounds escaping as the engine slows. Deborah sits next to me. 'Why do you say that?'

I flex my arms, which had begun to ossify. 'It's true. I did not argue with my mother.'

Deborah is nonplussed. 'But everyone knows about you and your mother. The way you stood up to her.'

'That was not a lifelong habit.'

Kimberley sighs and Deborah looks down, distracted. The dark bell of her hair falls forward. She makes no move to push it away. 'I wonder if she'll fight with me,' she muses.

'Will it be all right if she does?' I'm wriggling my toes, working against the tingling that's setting in. If I were to get to my feet now, I'd fall, I think.

'I hope so. I hope I don't try and sit on her opinions.' Her mouth slews sideways, self-deprecatingly. 'How's she going to turn out to be a great lawyer if she can't stand up for herself? It'd be interesting, actually, to have her stand up to me. I do know I can be a bit dogmatic. I suppose I'm too much for Mum, who's kind of squishy.'

'Your grandmother was the weak one. Your mother's stronger than you think.'

The light has been slowly fading. Inside I am sinking at the thought of driving home in the dark. It really is beyond me. A last shaft of setting sun arrows though the window, banding the table and forming a reservoir in the corner. The table looks like some giant sleeping animal. My hands have been transformed in this light, they have lost their palomino coat. Deborah's pale flesh has become rosy, her cream outfit glows softly.

She yawns. I worry about her, the hours she works, and now here she is at home with a baby to care for and no husband tonight to help. Peter is not due back from Melbourne until tomorrow evening. 'You didn't like Grandma much did you?' she asks.

'I liked Beth, but I thought, to use your word, that she was "squishy". I thought my brother could have done with someone stronger.'

'Mum loved her.'

'I should hope so.' I struggle to see something and then it comes to me. 'My mother was the opposite, too strong, but I loved her.'

Deborah yawns again. 'Here's hoping I get it right, like Goldilocks. Not too weak, and not too strong, but just right.'

'My dear, you're very tired. Can I help you with dinner?'

She half-laughs. 'We always get to this point. I'm half a century younger than you. How about I cook dinner for you?'

I have never stayed in the evening. Never. Perhaps it is time for me to change. I accept and Deborah, although surprised, rises to her feet with alacrity, passes Kimberley to me and sets about preparing the meal.

She cooks pasta (I called it spaghetti but was corrected) in the shape of little bows with three cheeses (none of which I've ever heard of) and fresh herbs. The cheese is a bit sticky on my dentures but I don't say anything. There's also a fresh salad, with greens I've not encountered before, but which are very tasty, and crusty bread rolls. I have to leave the crusty bits and eat the soft inside, which, although white, is surprisingly good. I don't eat bread with a meal, it's not compatible eating to ask your stomach to deal with the starch, and I most certainly don't eat white bread, but I am a guest in someone else's house and I feel very exotic blending in with this different environment.

It is now quite dark. Kimberley has woken once more and is gurgling to herself in her cot. Deborah lifts her out and holds her. I look at them across the litter of dinner plates, winking crystal, crushed napkins and food scraps. In the soft light burnishing the table to a rich sheen and their flesh to a golden hue, I see a madonna and child. In a moment of great joy I realise that it is just like one of those still lifes that I like so much, and that I can clearly see the source of light. I have just understood that it is reflected light which warms those dark paintings, and that lamps and candles are assumed beyond the frame. My heart knocks noisily in my chest. This small epiphany, granted to me by the Lord quite out of the blue, has winded me with excitement. Perhaps I am being rewarded for having taken a risk. I stir, without meaning to.

'Don't clear the table yet.' Deborah puts out a detaining hand.

'No.' Honesty seems called for. 'Normally I would. I'm not in the habit of sitting at the table once a meal is finished.'

'Always so busy.' Her tone is affectionate. 'Anyway, who am I to talk. I'm always on the go, in one way or another.'

'Just a different way to me.'

She leans forward, earnest now. 'Before dinner you said something about you and your mother, about standing up to her being a one-off. I know she was—I guess dominating's the right word—' I nod in agreement, 'but you wouldn't have been able to do what you did unless you'd developed some muscle.'

I like that term. Me, the date loaf supremo, secretly bulging with pectorals under my apron. 'My mother was dominating, but you have to understand, I didn't feel or know I was being overridden. It was natural to honour and obey my parents.'

'You can honour and obey what's reasonable but still know when it's unreasonable.'

'I didn't think of it in those terms. My mother's word was my command.'

'Was that true of all of you—your brothers too?'

My stomach contracts, with a truth I've not wanted to face. 'No, my brothers disagreed at times with Mum.'

'And survived,' Deborah comments.

'Mum loved William, with the strong feeling that I guess often goes to the firstborn. And James was the baby—we all had a soft spot for him.'

'I see,' she says sceptically, 'the boys were favoured.'

'It sounds like that but that's not really what happened.' This is very difficult for me. 'For Mum, her sons were obviously different, and she was proud of them for that. With me, it was more like I was a part of her, a part that was difficult to control. She was very proper, Mum, it was important to her.'

Deborah's frowning at me. 'What are you saying? That because she thought you were an extension of herself that she couldn't be proud of you? Only of boys, because they weren't like her?'

'Not exactly. Mum worked very hard to master herself, and she set the same high standards for me. It was work in the eyes of God, it was to show Him that she tried to live by His principles.'

'It sounds like she was a control freak to me.' Deborah sees me wince. 'Sorry. That was a bit rough.'

Suddenly I feel as if I could slip sideways off my chair, I'm so tired. The room blurs before me and I grip the seat of the chair with both hands to keep myself upright. Deborah says something but I don't catch it. She leans across the table.

'You're exhausted aren't you?'

'It's getting to my bedtime,' I confess.

Deborah consults her watch. 'Eight-thirty is your bedtime?' She puts Kimberley in her cot. 'No wonder you get up so early. Aunty you can't drive home.'

I hold on to the chair. 'No, I don't think I can.'

'You're going to stay the night. I'll tuck you up in the spare bedroom. Come on, on your feet and lively.'

I smile. 'I haven't heard that one for a while.'

'It's yours.' I must look uncertain because she says, 'I got it from you.'

'It's not mine originally.' We're climbing the stairs, slowly, and in my case, painfully. Making it to the top seems to be purely a matter of willpower.

I allow myself to be fussed over. I sit on the bed while Deborah fetches me a towel and washer and a nightgown. She even produces a toothbrush, still in its plastic-covered box.

'You can bring the cot in here tonight if you like,' I say.

Deborah pauses at the doorway. Leaning down to check one of her stockings she says, 'You know, I think I'll take her in with me tonight.' She raises her head. 'I've been thinking her room's a bit far away. I might have to do some rearranging.'

Hallelujah. After I've washed my face and cleaned my teeth I slip into the bed and fall back upon the pillow as if pushed. I'm too tired even to send up a vote of thanks for Deborah's decision concerning Kimberley. Tomorrow morning I'll wake to a strange room and I'll fret over the absence of fresh clothes, but tonight this strange bed is welcome. I don't find it easy to be taken care of, it's not something I've ever learnt, but tonight I am grateful. I have no slippers or dressing-gown waiting on a chair by the bed. My house waits for me, anxious and alone. There'll be no one to witness the glory of morning in my garden. I sink into the soft mattress, which is a bit too soft. That's Deborah, choosing luxury over practicality. I sink and sink and the last thought I'm conscious of is, on your feet and lively. I'm anything but, yet I smile as sleep comes to fetch me.

I dream of the Townleys, whom I've kept out of mind for

sixty years. In my dream they are on stage, putting on some vaudeville act; a very Townley sort of thing to do. The act is full of closed circuit references and jokes. It gets harder and harder to follow, while they fall about laughing more and more and more. At some point what was being offered for public entertainment becomes a show just for themselves, which excludes everybody else. I am straining forward in my seat, trying to make sense of the show. I look around and realise that I *am* the audience. There is no one else in the hollow auditorium. I look to the stage once more and at that point the Townleys all turn and jeer at me. The spotlight shifts and finds me perched on my solitary chair and I burn with shame under that hot light as the sound of the Townley's mockery ricochets off the walls.

I wake, sick at heart. I've overheated during the night and I can smell my sweat, sour under the sheets. It is still dark. I fumble aside the bedclothes and stand up, unsure of my surroundings. I can't remember where the window is, or the door. I take a step, with my hand out to feel the way, and I knock something hard. I steady it and feel that it is the bedside lamp. Illumination makes the world of difference. I survey the room. When I wake at dawn at home I feel as if my house wakes with me and together we greet the day. This morning I am conscious that I am awake in a sleeping house. My dream feels very close and I sense the currents of dreams still channelling through Deborah and Kimberley, swirling through the darkened rooms. Here I am the odd one out, not mistress of my domain but an interloper, a fugitive from sleep.

I strip the bed. Gathering the mound of linen I open the door and make my way downstairs. At the foot of the stairs the strangeness of my presence returns with force, as my bare feet chill on marble. I don't like it. I want my slippers. I turn on the hall light, then the dining room light, the kitchen light and finally, the laundry light. I bundle the sheets and pillow-cases into the washing machine and start the cycle. The back door is behind me, its glass pane revealing the grey shapes of things as form emerges from darkness. I can't even remember where the key is kept, although my hand reaches automatically to where my key at home hangs. Here there is only a blank wall, and my groping fingers.

Outside dawn is breaking. I'm up at the right time in the wrong house. I can see the dew on the paving stones through the glass. I couldn't go out there in bare feet. A sparrow lands on the stones and looks about at the cast iron garden furniture, the terracotta pots. The bird pecks uncertainly at a gap in the paving stones but there is no food there. It flies away. I know how it feels.

I put the kettle on, the tiles in the kitchen radiating a terrible coldness through the soles of my feet. I pull old newspaper from the recycling stack in the laundry and lay it across the kitchen floor. It's easier than going upstairs for my shoes. In my borrowed nightgown, with crumpled newsprint under my feet, I feel derelict. I make the tea and stand with my hands curled around the teapot for warmth. Tears of self-pity prick at the back of my eyes but I refuse to give in to them. I will borrow a blouse and fresh stockings from Deborah; I will be grateful that I need not go out, knowing that I do not have on clean underwear; I will return home this evening. I drink my tea.

It is all very well to have braced myself but I know that my dream has unsettled me. I feel faintly ill, knowing I must open the door to folk I've been ignoring for most of my life. What shocked me in the dream was the malice borne by the Townleys. Yet why should I be shocked? I treated them without kindness, having received much kindness from them. They were a family closed in upon themselves, more aware of each other than of the world outside. Yet what family is not like that? In the Townleys' case it was mixed up with performance for each other which, from my point of view, made them seem a family imbued with magic. I sat before them, admiring and applauding. I was so aware of my need for them that it did not occur to me that they needed me. They liked being the magic troupe, performing before my fascinated eyes.

I first met Marion Townley at the Red Cross, where we were training as volunteers in basic nursing skills. We were both twenty. This was a brave move for me, as I did not leave the house for the most part, except to do the shopping or attend meetings. I helped Mum run the house and worked hard to make our men comfortable. William had completed his apprenticeship and had gone on to work for an engineering company. Mr Lewis had sold the business to Dad and retired, first travelling around the world with his wife. We received postcards from foreign parts, which we looked up on the globe. Upon his return home Mr Lewis presented Mum with a fine English clock, a Woodbury, and he gave me a necklace of red beads. It was my pride and joy and when I wore it I felt foreign, Spanish perhaps.

Mum was not impressed with the idea of the Red Cross.

'They do such good work,' I pleaded.

'You have plenty of work right here at home.'

'I won't let that suffer Mum, I promise. I could be so helpful if I had nursing skills.'

'Helpful to whom? You're not traipsing around hospitals. Don't think for a minute that you are.'

I nodded vigorously. 'I wouldn't. I promise I wouldn't. I was thinking of the family.'

Mum set down her rolling pin. We were in the kitchen, on baking day. 'I've nursed this family through many a sickness. I nursed you back to life my girl. Are you saying that my skills are not good enough?'

I was horrified. 'No. Mum, no. I'd like to be able to offer what you do.' I had a moment of inspiration. 'Who's going to look after you if you get sick?'

'I don't get sick.' She started to knead the dough. It gave way, pliable under her fingers.

Disappointment seared me. 'I want to go.'

'Do you think we can all do just what we like?' Mum punched out scones, quickly and expertly. My bowl of cake mixture was settling into a soggy mess. 'You'd better hurry up with that cake. It's supposed to go into the oven at the same time as the scones.'

I started to beat but my heart wasn't in it. 'I don't ever go out. I spend all my time with the family.'

Mum emphatically punched out the last scone. 'What, I pray, is it about your family that you need to get away from?'

The thought came into my head, unbidden and shocking. You. I shied away from the table as if stung. My hand clipped the bowl and it crashed to the floor. The mixture spread thickly over the broken china.

'That was a four-egg cake,' Mum said, her lips thin. 'Not to mention the half pound of butter. It will come out of your allowance.'

I had a small allowance, to cover my tram fares for shopping. I started cleaning up the mess. 'I won't be able to get to the shops.'

'It was your hand broke the bowl, not mine.' She slid the tray of scones into the oven and snapped the door shut. I stayed on my knees, mopping up the viscous mixture and retrieving scraps of china. Even though I was careful a sharp sliver pierced my skin, under the fingernail. I started to bleed.

Against all caution I opened the topic again at tea that night. Putting down my knife and fork to better hold on to my apprehension I said to Dad, 'Mum and I have already discussed this, and she has said no, but I want to go to the Red Cross classes in nursing.'

Dad turned to Mum. 'What don't you like about the idea?'

'Annie has work to do at home.'

'My work won't suffer. I'll make sure all my jobs are done.'

I looked at Dad, ignoring Mum. 'Mum nursed me back to life, and she's nursed you. Don't you think it's a good idea for me to have nursing skills too?'

Dad nodded. 'Yes I do. Clara, where's the harm in it? It'll be good for the girl to get out a bit.'

Mum speared a piece of brawn. 'If that is your decision I'll abide by it.'

'It's not a decision. I'm suggesting it's a good idea.'

'You're the head of the household. If you think it's a good idea then so be it.'

Mum obviously didn't think it was a good idea. James was eating his tea, looking at the ceiling. There were only the four of us, William being at his fiancée, Beth's, for tea. I sat between Mum and Dad, dejection settling on my shoulders.

Mum was concentrating on her plate. Dad gave her an annoyed, frustrated look and then, surprisingly, said, 'Very well. If it's my decision, Annie can go. It'll do her good.'

Mum looked up then, her face stony. Dad raised an eyebrow at her. I was catapulting between ecstasy and terror. There was an interminable silence. Dad started eating again. Mum was doggedly working her way through her meal.

'When do the classes start?' Dad asked me.

'In two weeks.'

'It's a good skill to have. We hope you make the most of it, don't we Clara?'

Mum looked at me. 'Of course. Don't think it's an excuse to go gallivanting about. And say thank you to your father.'

'Thank you Dad.'

'Your mother and I both wish you the best,' Dad said.

Mum said, 'Eat your tea Annie. That's good brawn you're letting go to waste there.'

And so I arrived at Parramatta Town Hall. The Red Cross had the use of the main hall and I looked around with interest. The stage was hidden from view by heavy velvet curtains, crimson trimmed in yellow braid. The chairs normally used for seating were stacked against the walls, giving the room a fortified air. It was a relatively plain room, save for the vivid shock of curtain and the relief circling the walls up high, where narrow windows beyond the reach of human hands let in the light. They puzzled me, those windows, leaning forward into the room as if curious, until, one day when it started to rain, the instructor picked up a long pole leaning in a corner and, reaching up, tipped the glass back into vertical position.

'My goodness but you've got style,' were Marion's first words to me. She was struggling with the veil issued to volunteers.

'I beg your pardon?' I turned to see if there was someone behind me, but the other volunteers were scattered around the dressing room at odd intervals. I was closest to Marion. She was cheerful and stout, with the bob of the day completely unsuited to her broad face. She pointed to my head and blew through her lips, making a windy, exasperated sound. I had slipped my veil on and twisted up the stiff white mass to fashion a cloche bonnet. By tucking up the drop and pinning it flat to the back of my head I had made a neat cap. My heavy plait lay coiled underneath.

Marion's veil was sliding across her fringe, careering down the precipice of her forehead. She screwed her face up. 'How did you do it? I feel like mine's about to take flight.'

I edged forward. 'Would you like some help?'

'Please.' Her relief was evident.

I secured the veil in front but Marion's short hair left nothing to attach the drop of material to. She shrugged. 'I probably look like I'm off to my first communion but at least I can see.'

'You look like a proper nurse,' I said.

'That's kind of you. I'm sure I look a dreadful fright. I do in everything.' She smiled at me. Her teeth were very large and very white. 'If I had any real patients I'd probably scare them to death.'

'They'd think you were an angel of mercy,' I remonstrated.

Marion put her hand on my arm. 'You really are kind.' I was unused to being touched and her hand felt strange and heavy. I didn't know whether to brush it away, like a fly, or whether I was required to reciprocate. I didn't know what to do with that hand. Marion hooted, 'I can hardly wait to tell my family. An angel of mercy—good grief!' She took her hand away and I cradled my arm, as if it had been damaged.

In the large hall we stood in rows behind long trestle tables on which were stacked rolls of bandages, pins and pans the shape of kidney beans. Everyone was dressed in white. A surge of awe shook me. This was the good work indeed. The woman at the front raised her pointer and I tipped my face to the ornate ceiling, expecting music to rise from every throat, a confluence of voices lifted in praise.

Something was tugging at my left sleeve. Marion was leaning towards me, pink skin shiny across her nose. I could see freckles, pale and tiny, caught under the net of skin. 'Deaf to the world you were. Off with the pixies.' Marion presented a face of intense concentration to the front of the room yet was talking to me. I was turning to look at her, visibly distracted. 'Don't look at me,' she whispered. 'Watch the teacher.' I did, and Marion kept talking. I had seen girls do this at school and had never understood how they could carry on a private conversation whilst following the lesson. Now I was doing it. 'I bet we have to wrap each other up in those bandages,' Marion hissed. 'We'll look like mummies at the end of the day.'

I smiled. I couldn't remember smiling in class before. 'And those pans worry me,' continued Marion. 'What if they're our lunch dishes as well—economy of materials and all that?'

I was light of heart. Giddy with new sensation. 'Why are you here?' I whispered, and would not have been surprised to have been told it was a visitation.

'Mum thought I'd better learn something useful. She reckons it's a good idea to have some skills.' She became serious. 'Nice to think you could help.' The pointer at the front of the hall knocked with purpose against a blackboard. Shoes were sliding softly over floorboards as the standing volunteers shifted their weight from one leg to the other and moved their limbs to relieve the dense mass of themselves pressing like gravity. Uniforms rustled. 'What about you?' Marion asked.

My secret wish was to save lives, but it was not to be spoken of. 'I'd like to take care of people.' I looked directly at Marion. 'As you said, nice to be able to help.'

The pointer tapped and silence ensued, the rustling bodies stilled. The instructor was looking at me, an enquiring expression on her face. I'd been caught talking in class. I was mortified and felt the hot, slow stain of my shame spread across my neck and face. I murmured an apology and the class resumed. Marion took my hand and squeezed it. Commiseration and cameraderie. It was more than worth the humiliation.

We took our places next to each other at every class. Marion's bandaging was adequate, workmanlike, but I revealed a gift for placing the lengths of white crepe, for securing them so that they supported but did not disturb, for holding the damage at precisely its weakest point.

'Beats me how you do it with those hands,' Marion observed.

I didn't know where to place my hands. They seemed unaccountably larger than ever.

'Sorry,' she grimaced. 'You've got a thing about them, haven't you?' She took my hands and placed them palm to palm against her own. 'Look, your hands are bigger than mine,' she nodded to the table at our side, 'but your work is so much finer. I envy that.'

The warmth of any skin except my own was unfamiliar. In the two weeks I'd known Marion she had touched me more often than had my father in a lifetime, if I didn't count the stiff brushing of moustache against my temple which counted as kisses on special occasions.

'Don't feel bad about your hands when they can do work like that.' Marion pulled a piece of crepe towards her. 'Is everything you do as good?'

My tongue stumbled. 'I was sick as a child and had time to practise—knitting or sewing or anything detailed. But my work is nothing special; my mother's is much better.'

Marion hooked her thumbs into her belt. 'I've never really been sick.'

I could not doubt it. There were no rivers of disturbance cutting deep gorges in Marion, no need for her to carve a place to hide. Someone so open to God would live in a body cleansed of sin.

'I've always been ill.' I looked away, ashamed.

'You poor chook. Your mum must worry about you.'

'I'm a terrible trial to my mother.' I smoothed my apron. 'She prays for my soul.'

Marion's eyes were bright under her fringe. 'It's not your soul I'd be worrying about if I was your mum. Anyway,' she flicked my fingers, 'these are gifted hands. Show me again how you do the shoulder bandage.'

At home Mum was unimpressed. 'It's all very well for you to be full of yourself, Miss, but you should spare a thought for the sin of pride.'

It didn't feel like pride. It felt like something that I couldn't give a name to, not ever having known it before. I had never had a friend like Marion, with goodness shining right through her. I didn't know why she was content to be my friend. I was afraid to ask, as if questioning it might cause it to slip away.

William asked. 'You seem happy these days.' I had brought him lunch, where he was painting the shed.

I lifted my head in stunned recognition. 'Yes, I am. Happy.' The word soared off my tongue. 'I have a new friend.'

William leant back against the ladder, his sandwich in one fist. 'At the Red Cross?' I nodded. 'Has this person got a name?'

'Marion.' Her name was an offering. 'Marion Townley.'

'Good for you. Why don't you invite her home for supper?' I must have looked doubtful because he quickly said, 'Better still, why don't you do something with her after class?'

'Do what?'

'Go for a walk. Buy an ice-cream. Go shopping.'

'I don't think Marion would want to help with the grocery shopping.'

'No you goose. Shopping, for fripperies.'

'For what?'

'Ribbons and things. I'm not sure exactly. Beth and her sister go shopping together. They have a lot of fun.'

I didn't need any ribbons but I didn't point that out. Instead I thanked him, more so when Marion invited me to a concert. He'd opened up possibilities for me and I was able to say yes. Only on the way home did I wonder what I would tell Mum. Music, if not the plain-song of ordinary folk raised in praise of the Lord, was trespass.

When I was younger I had asked Mum why our meeting had no organ. 'The world is attractive to the flesh and the Devil is always whispering to Christians about it, making attractive offers with plausible explanations,' had been Mum's response.

'An organ is an offer from the Devil?' I had guessed.

'Make melody in your heart to the Lord, giving thanks for all things. None other is pure.'

I decided not to tell Mum. I made the decision in my room before tea. I sat on my bed, facing the wardrobe, a dark, heavy cupboard with one tall door attached to a smaller set of drawers. A narrow, practical cupboard. My room was painted the colour of vellum, which in certain lights seemed creamish, and in others was green-tinged and distasteful. The coverlet on my bed, with its spartan wrought iron bedhead, was white. A washstand stood against the wall between the bed and cupboard, its marble top a mottled grey. The jug and bowl were of thick plain china, also white. The curtains at the window were white, the hook rug on the bare boards an indeterminate colour.

I was narrow and practical, like my wardrobe. I didn't have to be like that. I had a choice.

'On Saturday, there is a class,' I announced at dinner. 'An afternoon class.'

'What sort of people are they to organise classes on Saturday?'

I shrugged. 'I'll do all my jobs in the morning. I'll leave at two o'clock.'

Mum clicked her tongue. 'A weekend, and so close to the Sabbath. What do you think Walter?'

'It's the Red Cross,' Dad said. 'I'm sure they know what they're doing.'

James piped up. 'Can I come?'

'No,' I answered quickly, so quickly that everyone looked at me. 'It'd be boring for you. We stand there, folding bandages. After five minutes you'd wish you weren't there.'

'Is that how you feel?' Mum asked.

'No, but James would. Folding bandages is no good for an eleven-year-old boy.'

I was far from comfortable. Mum's searching, so close to my conscience, was nudging me toward confession. She gave a firm nod, pushed her glasses back up onto the bridge of her nose and said, 'You may go.'

On Saturday I stood in front of my mirror adjusting my hat. My hand shook as I twisted the bone-tipped hat pin through a knot of hair. Perfidy pulsed in my blood. I had lied to my mother, was continuing the lie even as I secured my hat. I stared at myself, at my wayward eye and doubt shaded cheek. I had the look of a sinner. The sampler my mother had stitched for my last birthday hung next to the mirror, set there to keep me from vanity. *Be sure your sins will find you out*, red and blue intricate cross-stitch spelt out. I turned it to face the wall.

The gate latch clicked to behind me. I had left the fold. The sky above was a pitiless blue, with me an ant exposed to it. The house was blank at my back, its doors and windows recording my exit. I walked away slowly, my shoulders stiff and wary, and stumbled, having difficulty holding myself straight. I reached the corner and the house no longer had me in its sights, but the hollow between the wings of my shoulders still tingled. I expected angels of retribution to alight before me on the road, ribbons of fire issuing from their mouths. Instead a tram clanged around the corner. I mounted the stairs, paid my fare and sat, clenched and shocked.

At Parramatta I walked downhill to the town hall, strong emotion propelling me like a hand at my back. I passed the sandstone church which sits across the street from the town hall, its back turned to its larger brother. I stopped, my shadow behind me. I turned and half ran to the open door. I stood on the threshold of the Anglican church and then I took a step forward, into the hushed gloom. My eyes did not adjust at first and I stood there, blind and uneasy, with the most curious sensation of swaying. Shapes began to emerge from the blackness and I saw that I stood at the foot of a red carpeted aisle, stretching from the toes of my shoes to the altar at the far end of the church. Rows of seats in polished wood lined the aisle. I stepped forward, my heels making no sound on the carpet. In the rows what looked like small Bibles lay on shelves tucked under the seats. One of the little blue-covered books lay on the seat and I leant down and picked it up. It opened naturally to a page about one third of the way in and I brought the volume up close to my face. It was not a Bible. It seemed to be some sort of prayer but I didn't recognise it. I turned the page, then another, and another. All prayers, none of which I knew. I realised that I'd stopped breathing; was in fact holding my breath. I gulped in air and put the book with its foreign prayers down. Brightly coloured lozenges of light lay scattered over wood and carpet. I looked up to see Christ with his arms raised in benediction. When I turned He was hanging from the Cross, blood trickling down from His crown of thorns.

I had looked at the windows of St John's many times, noting that the glass was coloured, wondering about the bands of iron crazing the expanses. But from the outside no light pulsed behind the colours and I had not known these windows were depictions of the Son of God. I had not known they were so extraordinary. I moved into a swirl of blue light, lifted my hand and it caught red fire. This was not plain. This was not at all plain. This was beautiful.

A woman appeared through an arched doorway at the side of the building carrying a large vase of flowers. A second woman, also carrying flowers, followed her. They smiled at me and arranged the vases on pedestals at the foot of the stairs leading to the altar. They murmured to each other as they stepped back to appraise the positioning. They each had a rag tucked into an apron pocket, and one of them pulled her rag out and buffed the brass candlestick standing near the pedestal. I looked past them to the altar and saw that there was brass everywhere, in the rails protecting the altar, in candlesticks tall and short, in the bookrest standing on the stone plinth at the front of the church. I didn't know what that plinth was for. It looked imposing.

I backed out until I stood in the stone-flagged foyer. Then I turned and blinked into the street. The town hall clock struck the hour and I ran down the side of the church, across to the entrance of the hall, to where I could see Marion anxiously watching out for me.

'Sorry,' I said.

She grabbed my hand. 'Quick. We'll just have time to take our seats.'

We trotted inside and made our way into the middle of the auditorium. The orchestra was tuning, the audience shuffling and clearing throats. The spread of colour in the stained glass windows lay over everything I saw like a fine lens. It clung to surfaces, defined planes, lay like mesh on skin. Inside I was rising like bread, a swollen happiness stretching my chest. I turned to Marion. She was staring at the painted ceiling, chewing her lip. Her hands, busy in her lap as if unconnected to the rest of her, were steepling themselves. It was a game of castles without anyone to admire it. She felt me looking, and her hands froze mid-game. She winked at me and turned her hands palm up, to rest on her thighs. We turned our attention to the front and the music began.

The tea is cold. Cold and stewed. The smell of tannin is strong as I empty the rest of the pot down the sink. I catch the tea leaves in a sieve but have to empty that into the garbage bin. Deborah does not have a container for food scraps. There is no compost bin in that elegant courtyard.

I wash my cup and saucer, retrieve the newspaper from the floor and return it to its bin. There is now no trace of me. When I die it will be the same. My house will be sold, my possessions divided amongst obscure members of the family (I can't imagine that there is anything of mine that Deborah may want) and even my vegetable beds will probably be turned under for flowers. There are no children, in whom it would be possible to discern a curve of cheek or a mannerism or mode of speech. My morbidity does not impress me. It was Deborah after all who told me to be on my feet and lively, just last night. It's probably time to sort through my photographs and see if there are any that Deborah would like. That one of my parents in the buggy, she might like that one. Or that one of my mother, a fresh young beauty. She may even like one of me.

The cycle on the washing machine clicks to a halt. I transfer the laundry to the dryer and turn the dial. I wouldn't use a dryer myself; there's an odour that comes with laundry that never sees the light of day. Often I've stood in the backyard with my nose pressed to the linen in my arms. You can smell sunshine in laundry, it's a marvellous thing. I watch the sheets dutifully heave and flop in the dryer and look through the back door at the poor excuse for a clothesline. Many are those who have no backyard, only a courtyard, or a poor thin balcony tacked onto a unit. Sydney's full of people who've never known the pleasure of gathering in the washing, grass underfoot and sky in your eyes and the feeling of daylight in your arms.

'Morning Aunty. Did you sleep well?'

Deborah is in some glamorous nightgown and robe but her face is soft and a little crumpled with sleep. She looks extraordinarily young and pretty. It's been years since I've seen her without make-up.

'You're standing on the slate in bare feet. Look at your poor feet.'

They're a little blue, it's true. I've been a little blue all over this morning, but only my feet are showing it.

'Come into the dining room.' She holds out her hand to me. 'Come on.'

I follow her and she sits me down in a chair, kneels before me and places my feet on her lap. She takes one foot between her palms and starts to gently rub, her hands coaxing warmth and circulation. My feet are far from pretty; they're gnarled, well used. I've a bunion that's been threatening for twenty years on my right foot. Sitting there, with Deborah's warm hands on my raddled flesh, her head bent to the task, I feel the urgency of tears press at the back of my eyes. It's Mary and Christ, of course, that Deborah has discovered for us. I'm so grateful I could kiss her. This is how the Bible meets every need, gives meaning to every part of life. This is how the Word becomes flesh.

'There,' she says. 'That's better.'

And of course it is better. My feet no longer have the look of dead fish and the morbidity which has assailed me all morning has lifted.

'Thank you,' I say, and the tone of my voice must have hinted at the morning's distress because she looks at me sharply then, rising to her feet, leans forward and kisses me on the forehead.

'No worries,' she says. 'What about some breakfast? Do you want to shower first?'

Upstairs I chuckle at my reflection when I have finished dressing. The borrowed blouse is pure silk, with graceful shoulder yoking. 'Just something I throw on at weekends,' Deborah had told me, to quell my anxiety. It feels like half a ball gown to me. And looks it, against my plaid skirt. The stockings feel like silk too, and are far more sheer than the matt ones I normally wear. I turn my ankle for myself in the mirror, a cheesecake pose. I don't think that sheer stockings and sensible shoes are a good combination. My clumpers lend themselves more to support stockings.

When I arrive in the kitchen again Deborah has already fetched down Kimberley and our reflections bouncing off fridge and cupboard door almost make the room cosy. Soon Hilary will bring Hugo round, her nanny having some appointment today that makes her unavailable. We'll create a family atmosphere yet.

Deborah eyes my outfit. 'That's not a good look Aunty.'

'No, it isn't.'

'You didn't have any plans did you? To go out?'

'No. I intend only to provide fodder for Hilary's disdain.'

Deborah laughs. 'That's un-Christian.'

'Not at all. I'm supporting a sister in her need.'

She laughs again and taps me on the hand with the egg slide. 'There's a wicked streak in you. Whoever said you were meek and mild?'

'I don't know. Who did?'

She raises an eyebrow but says nothing. She arranges eggs and toast on plates and we carry them into the dining room. Deborah brings in Kimberley, who's singing to herself. I eat my food, thinking what a difference tone makes. I've been called wicked before, but only this morning did I believe that it could be done affectionately.

I sit with Kimberley after breakfast, while Deborah dresses upstairs. The house is very quiet. Kimberley is blowing bubbles, endlessly delighted with the movement of her lips and the mushy sound. She smiles at me. I smile back. Everyone is biased in favour of their own baby, but Kimberley is very prepossessing. She's a pretty child, with smoothly textured skin and a dark promise of hair. We are three generations apart, she and I. I am from the beginning of this century and she's been born near its close. History has found us, in this terrace house in Sydney, bridging one hundred years of modernity. When I am with her I am aware of the baton which is passed from one generation to the next. This is a life, take it, it's yours. Use it well and pass it on. History is full of truncations, where the baton was dropped, or fumbled, withheld or snatched violently away. I was a fumbler myself, and yet here is Kimberley. She burbles at me, little starfish hands clutching at air. Use it well, pass it on.

A flood tide of grief surges through me. I did not use my life well. I have not passed it on. Once again I am a handmaid to life. Small bubbles line Kimberley's lips, a little string of ephemera she has created all by herself. I stroke the downy scalp. The handmaid is an honourable position.

Street noises are beginning to filter into the homely peace. A neighbour's car starts up, chokes, fires again. A woman's voice calls out, clear and intimate. 'Harold,' she calls. 'Harold.' Husband, child, dog? Impossible to tell.

I clear the breakfast table, talking to Kimberley all the while. Deborah comes in, polished in oyster grey. She picks Kimberley up, dangles her in the air, murmuring endearments. Kimberley smiles and burbles. I don't think I've ever seen Deborah pick Kimberley up once she's dressed for work. She will move the cot, will lean over it and touch Kimberley from that safe distance, but she doesn't cuddle her of a morning. Cuddles are reserved for the evening. Today she holds her baby on her shoulder, while sorting through her handbag for something, and the inevitable happens. Kimberley dribbles milk and saliva onto Deborah's jacket and the little back shudders as if ready to bring up more. I run over and put a tea towel on Deborah's shoulder and Kimberley heaves once, twice.

I take away the warm, steaming towel. Deborah kisses Kimberley on the top of her head. 'Thank you Kimbles, for that mark of your esteem. Back in the cot for you.'

I fetch a cloth and clean the mess on Deborah's jacket. The wet stain is a toadstool on the pale fabric. 'Do you want to change?' I ask.

Deborah is surprisingly unperturbed. 'No. This will dry. Besides, I quite like the idea of catching a whiff of Kimberley throughout the day. Clients can think it's my new perfume.'

Good for you, I think. I dab at the wet patch. 'This might leave a bit of a water mark.'

Deborah shrugs. The front door closes and we hear Marla approaching from the hallway. Deborah says, 'It was good having you stay last night.'

'It was good of you to have me to stay. Thank you for looking after me.'

She turns to face me. 'I mean it was good for me. I slept more easily having someone else in the house, and it was nice to wake up to someone, to have breakfast with someone.'

'Miss Grace. So early!' It is Marla, very surprised. 'You fly here now in morning?'

'Aunty slept here last night to help me out. Marla, will you change my sheets today. I know I'm throwing out the schedule but I'd like clean sheets tonight.'

'I've got a load in the dryer,' I remember.

'No worries,' Marla says. I like it when she plays tough with our expressions.

The doorbell rings and Deborah goes to let Hilary in. Hilary must be in a tearing hurry because Deborah returns carrying Hugo and a carry-all. Hugo looks bewildered. Marla reaches for him and for the bag and disappears into the living room.

'Hilary was in a great rush,' I comment.

'Hilary's always in a great rush when she's alone with Hugo,' Deborah drily remarks. 'She can't wait to pass him on to someone else.' I look at her. She shrugs. 'She's my friend, she makes me laugh, but I don't think she's cut out for motherhood.'

I wipe down the table. Deborah reaches down and smooths a hand over Kimberley's scalp. Straightening, she applies lipstick, fishes out her keys and looks around blankly. She can't quite leave.

'Goodbye babycakes,' I say.

She gives me a smile like a Christmas tree, angel on top. Then she's gone, high heels a percussion beat on the courtyard stones.

Marla comes back and asks if I let anyone know I was not going to be at home last night. Maggie will have noticed the darkened house and could well be imagining the worst. I phone her while Marla strips Deborah's bed. It's a strange feeling, phoning my neighbour to tell her that I stayed out. An adolescent, almost rebellious feeling. I think I expect to get into trouble for my actions.

Well I might. It has been my experience that staying out causes trouble. At Parramatta Town Hall, as the noise of applause quickened the air and my palms stung from clapping, Marion leant across and asked if I wanted to go back to her place for tea. The music I had just been amazed by, the vision of stained glass which seemed to float before me throughout the concert and the presence of my new and remarkable friend all conspired to help me make an instant decision. I said yes. Yes, I repeated, and was almost immediately unnerved by a great shudder of fear. With effort I put that fear aside and fell back into the embrace of the music and the coloured glass. Marion was looking around discontentedly. She stood quickly.

'Come on. Let's get out before the crowd.'

I jumped to my feet. Marion was already in the aisle and I had to hurry to keep up with her. She didn't wait for me and I lagged behind her until we reached the wide sweep of the front entrance. I felt stupid. I wasn't sure if she wanted me to accompany her home. Maybe she had asked for the sake of politeness and had expected me to decline the invitation. I couldn't ask. I simply hovered, miserable and large. We walked up the street without speaking. At the tram stop Marion said, 'I'm not being much fun.'

'I don't have to come with you,' I got out.

'It's fine.' She glared down the street. 'That crowd really annoyed me.'

I nodded, without understanding. We boarded the tram, uneasiness still pickling our skins. We sat in silence, but as we entered streets I was unfamiliar with Marion began to point out buildings that had shaped her life; her old primary school, her best friend's house from high school, the chimney in the distance which belonged to her piano teacher's house. The metallic taste of discord began to fade.

Marion's house sat square in its garden, a dark purple brick with white trim. It was the new style of house, the Californian bungalow. The street was full of similar houses, all leaning against the evening sky like raw country folk scrubbed fresh for church. The gardens were not long established, although each house sported its handkerchief of grass between fence and front door, and rose beds under the fence. The front paths were of concrete. There was a shortage of trees.

I followed Marion along the driveway by the side of the house. The grass was patchy here and the ground rutted and I had to watch my step. A garage to match the house took almost half the space in the backyard, where a clothesline occupied central position. The only tree was a lemon tree and the yard was bare of shrubs or flowers. There was only the trimmed grass, the paling fence and the paling sky.

I stepped into the kitchen. A scrubbed wooden table held centre stage, yellow linoleum created a pool of warmth. A woman turned from the oven, whose heat had left her broad face flushed and moist. She wiped her hands on her apron and looked from Marion to me.

'So you're Annie. Marion's been talking of you such a lot, and we've been wondering when we'd meet you.'

I swam forward into the warmth of that kitchen and that welcoming smile. In my head Mrs Townley's words seemed tinged with disapproval, as if my absence had been deliberate. Yet her plump white throat and big-toothed smile, so like her daughter's, belied this thought.

She ushered me to a chair. My skin rippled with contentment, as a cat's does when caressed. 'Tea's not too far off but I'm sure you girls could do with a cuppa.'

'Mum, I'll make it.'

'No love, you sit there next to Annie and tell me all about the concert. Did you like it Annie?'

'She hasn't even had a chance to take her hat off.' Marion pulled me to my feet. 'We'll be back in two shakes.'

Marion led me into the hallway, where an oak hat stand swallowed the light edging through the pane of glass above the front door. Dark picture rails and skirting boards defined the walls. At first, leaving the warmth and light of the kitchen, my contentment had flickered. I had not sought permission to stay nor had I informed my mother of where I was. Panic rose in me in the gloom of the hallway. As I looked around my ease rekindled. The space was almost identical to ours. It was as if I were at home. There could be no objections to my being here.

'Do you need to pay a visit?' Marion asked. I shook my head. 'I do. You right to find your way back?'

I looked at my reflection in the hat stand mirror. My face was soft, with no trace of anxiety. Mrs Townley had been so welcoming. I had obviously been spoken of, but good things seemed to have been said of me. I turned my head to see myself from another angle. I looked almost pretty today. I took off my hat and leaning towards the mirror bit my lips for colour. When I straightened a young man was standing by the far wall. His eyes met mine in the mirror.

'You must be Marion's friend.'

My face was hot. 'I'm Annie Seeds.'

'Pleased to meet you. I'm Marion's brother, Tom.'

'Tom Townley,' I said, and blushed again.

'It's got a good ring to it, hasn't it?' He grinned and was so like his sister in that moment that I felt I knew him. He walked me back to the kitchen. 'Do you live nearby?'

'At Baulkham Hills. We used to live at Mays Hill but it got too built out.'

'It's changed a lot hasn't it, since we were young.' We entered the kitchen and Tom put a hand on my shoulder. 'Look who I found.'

Marion banged through the back door. 'You two have met then?'

Tom took his hand from my shoulder. I stood pinned to the spot and speechless from having had that hand on my shoulder. I had never been touched familiarly by any man outside the family.

Mrs Townley ineffectually patted some stray hair into place.

'I'll be dishing up soon. Do you girls still want that cup of tea?'

'I'll put the kettle on,' Marion said.

Tom pulled a chair out from the table for me.

'So, did you like the concert Annie?' Mrs Townley cracked an egg into a bowl.

I closed my eyes and thought of the music I had just heard. Heavenly music. I had felt transported. I opened my eyes to find Tom studying me curiously. 'It was wonderful,' I said.

'What were they playing?' Mrs Townley wanted to know.

'I don't know. I've never been to a concert before.'

Marion clattered some cups and saucers onto the table. 'It was Mozart. Divine. The pianist was very good.'

Tom said, 'Mozart's just right for your first concert.'

I thought so too. Mrs Townley lay down the eggbeater, threw back her head and began to sing. I did not recognise the music, but I recognised the clear beauty of the voice. The voice erased the broken egg shells, the reddened hands and Mrs Townley's homely face. It set everything in crystalline order, unravelled chaos, threw light.

Mrs Townley stopped singing and the kitchen reasserted itself. I found my hands placed together, in the attitude of prayer. The kettle whistled and Marion poured boiling water into the teapot. 'Mum passed lots of things onto me but not her voice. It's good isn't it?'

'You are blessed.' I heard the reverence in my voice.

'I am blessed with more than my voice.'

Marion and Tom winked at each other and pointed to themselves. 'She means us,' Marion said in a stage whisper.

Mrs Townley spun the handle on the eggbeater then peered into the bowl. 'That will do.' She turned with the bowl to the bench where she poured its contents over slices of bread and butter arranged in a dish.

Despite this being a relatively new house, there was something shabby about the kitchen. There were dirt marks on the cupboards and a scuff of black along a wall where chairs had been pushed up against it. The floor could have done with a polish. I furtively examined my teacup, which was tannin stained. Sternness gathered inside me. It was all very well to enjoy music but the kitchen was slightly dirty. My mother would never have allowed her kitchen to be in such a state.

Marion sat down and poured the tea. 'You would have enjoyed the concert Mum. You should have come.'

'There'll be other concerts.'

'You can sing to yourself,' I said.

Mrs Townley smiled. 'I often do.'

Tom tilted in his chair. The back rest touched the wall. 'We could put on a concert. Mum can be the star attraction, we'll put on our glad rags, won't we Marion, you can do the piano.' Marion pulled a face. 'We'll rope Bill in and charge the neighbours a florin.'

'Tom,' said Mrs Townley, scandalised.

He grinned. 'All right, we won't charge the neighbours. What do you think?' he asked Marion, who was nursing her tea cup in both hands. 'Do you think we'll get Bill to give us a tune?'

'What am I being organised for now?' A tall lanky man entered the kitchen and crossed it to place a kiss on Mrs Townley's cheek.

'We're going to put on a concert in the front parlour. Mum's going to do Wagner—'

'Thomas, I will do no such thing.'

'—and Marion's going to recite—what are you going to recite?'

'*The Lady of Shalott*,' Marion said, in dramatic fashion, her hands clasped at her breast.

'Very nice. Very tasteful. You, my boy, are going to sing.'

The tall man leant against the sink. He was all joints, quite different to Tom and Marion and his mother. 'I think I'd rather recite something too.'

Tom's grin was big enough to crack his face. 'What were you thinking of?'

'That poem, you know the one, about daffodils.'

Tom was delighted. 'A grand choice. Give us a line now, to rehearse a bit.'

Bill put a hand on his chest and stood to attention. In a sonorous voice he declaimed, 'I wandered lonely as a cloud.'

Marion leapt to her feet and stood on her chair, heels scraping the wood. 'Through the noises of the night, She floated down to Camelot.'

Mrs Townley took a deep breath and trilled a triumphant chord, redolent of the Valkyries.

Tom put his hands together. 'Bravo. Bravo.' I stood and joined him, applause cracking the air between my palms. The kitchen pulled a veil over the theatre and I sat. 'That was the best concert I've ever been to.' My smile was generally directed, the smile of a blind person.

Tom leant forward. 'I would think you're the best audience we've ever had. Besides, it's only your second concert.'

Marion clambered down and began gathering the tea things. Mrs Townley introduced her other son to me, then sent Marion to fetch her father from his workshed. Mr Townley was loosely strung together, like his elder son. He carved the roast after grace, his blade familiar at the bone.

'How's the table coming along Dad?' Tom shook his napkin into his lap, a white drift against the blue serge of his trousers.

'Coming along nicely. I'll turn one of the legs tomorrow.' He picked up the platter of pumpkin, potatoes and carrots. 'Is your father interested in carpentry?' he asked me.

'No. He's a gardener.'

'Ada, did you hear that? Now wouldn't you like that of me?'

'Are all your greens fresh from the garden then?' Mrs Townley asked. At my nod she said, 'That's a wonderful thing, to feed your family from the garden.'

Bill said, 'I notice we're starving.'

'Dad's making a cedar dining table for Mum,' Marion said.

I was impressed. Mr Townley laughed. 'We can't eat it but we can eat from it.'

Tom poured more gravy. 'Can I give you a hand tomorrow?' he asked his father.

'I'll turn the first leg and if it works you can have a go on the next one.'

'Is it difficult to turn a leg?' I asked.

Marion's hand went to the hem of her skirt. 'I could show you if you like.'

Mrs Townley tapped her on the back of her hand. 'Finish your dinner, Ruby Keeler.'

I didn't know who Ruby Keeler was. Bill must have seen my bewilderment, because he said, 'You know, the movie actress, the dancer.'

That made nothing clearer. 'Don't you go to the pictures?' Tom asked.

I shook my head. I wanted to say that moving pictures were sinful, an indulgence of the flesh, but the thoughts slid away in my mind. My mother would have had no trouble denouncing the practice, but then it was not my mother seated at the Townley's table breaking bread with them. More specifically, eating their bread.

'Would you like to go some time?' Tom was still watching me.

Marion broke in. 'I don't think Annie's mother—'

'I'd like to go to the pictures, thank you.'

Marion shot me a surprised squinty look. Her eyes flicked to her brother. I had stopped breathing. I took a ragged breath and then nodded at Tom, still watching me, to let him know it really was all right.

After tea I helped with the dishes. Tom and Marion decided to escort me to the tram and we set out, our shoes on the footpath sounding distinct in the night air. Marion placed herself in the middle and linked arms with me and Tom. 'My two favourite people,' she said. 'Look at the Milky Way. It's so clear tonight.'

We stood, heads back, the white light of moon and stars and the depthless black of sky washing us down. The Southern Cross was flung across a corner. In the distance a dog barked once, twice. Marion repeated, in a dreamy voice, 'My two favourite people,' and then we set off again in unison, our footsteps keeping perfect time on the concrete.

My tram stop was at the end of my street. The sky no longer seemed littered with light. I was very conscious of the lateness of the hour, of arriving home in the dark. I grew heavier with each step, a leaden mass trudging up the street. I tried to recall the stained glass, the music, Tom's face. Perhaps I'd made it all up.

I closed the front door behind me and there was Mum, lit from behind by the glow spilling from the living room. I had an image of Dad in his armchair, reading by the light of the standard lamp, safe and enclosed. I was beginning to feel too big for the hallway, as if I would smash objects with my elbows if I moved down its length. The white painted hat rack would topple, gouging holes in the opposite wall. The fern on the pedestal opposite the living room door would spill dirt on the runner. I would try to disappear into the deeper patches of blackness which were the doorways but they would shrink back before me.

Mum stood ramrod straight, staring at me. Her hair was neatly pinned back, her dress, even at the end of the day, fell in neat clean folds on her small frame. My large bones, my blowsy flesh were like a smell in the narrow space. I shifted my handbag from one arm to the other. Mum said nothing.

'Hello Mum.' The silence extended, it lay like a musty blanket between us. I was sure that my mother, immaculate and starched, could see the soiled film of a day away from home on my skin. My stockings had a ladder where I'd snagged them on the wooden chair in the concert hall. My mother had powers of sight. The void of night at my back would not deter her. She could see, I knew it.

'Marion's family invited me to eat with them.' Mum remained silent. 'I ate dinner at Marion's.'

'We waited for you. Our food was spoiled.'

I searched for words. 'It was spontaneous. I didn't know I was going to eat there.'

'Spontaneous is a fancy name for not thinking of others.'

I knew I was in the wrong, but it seemed an abstract proposition that had little to do with me. My chest was tight, my jaw held.

Mum stepped forward. 'You feel no remorse do you?' My set face gave her the answer and she turned on her heel and walked away toward the back of the house. I looked at my hands and saw that I was trembling. Yet the stoniness around my heart seemed immoveable. I clutched my handbag and followed my mother.

'William has stayed to eat at Beth's house without notice,' I pointed out.

Mum was furious. 'How dare you. Beth is William's fiancée.'

My thoughts clouded. 'I know, I mean, I know it's not the same, Marion being a friend—'

'It is *not* the same and yet you raise it as justification.'

'No, I only meant—it seems to me—I'm twenty Mum, and I do have friends.'

'You will not keep them if you treat those close to you without respect.' She looked at me with patent disgust. 'Sometimes I wonder how it is that you are of the same flesh and blood as me. Now go and apologise to your father for spoiling his tea. There's nothing more to be said.'

I retreated to the hall, still clutching my handbag like a sacrificial offering. Mum was right of course, yet the feeling of clamped refusal persisted. I stood in the hallway, in confusion. Mum was putting things away in a cupboard in the room behind me, and I inched down the hall, keeping close to the wall. Mum was right, and yet I had accepted an invitation tonight to go to the pictures and I had no intention of telling her. I wasn't going to apologise to Dad either. I went to my room and closed the door behind me. I looked in the mirror as I took off my hat. The fever spots on either cheek were back. I hung my jacket over the mirror. For the first time in my life I did not say my prayers before going to sleep.

My mother had an opal ring which she wore to meetings. It had been her mother's. It had a flaw, quite large, a milky patch shot through with pink in the corner of the ice-sharp blues and greens. It wasn't really a corner of course, the ring being oval. I sat staring at my mother's ring at the meeting the following morning, watching its colours glint and spark as she raised her hands in prayer. I was just like that flaw. My parents had created a family in the eye of God, transparent to His gaze, brilliantly coloured in faith. I was clouding it with wilfulness.

The meeting room was sparsely decorated, a hall used by different groups for various purposes. We'd had to find another hall after the old one was destroyed. This one did not belong to us either. It stood in a bare paddock, the only tree a scraggy gum out the front, whose shade was never enough for more than one car. The hall was painted white, inside and out, and with its tin roof and lack of shelter, in summer it was a furnace to sit in. From a distance it danced jerkily on its hillside, perpetually heat hazed. Unpolished wooden floors inside were regularly scrubbed clean by brethren womenfolk. Bare windows gave onto bare sky. Unmatched wooden chairs, two trestle tables and an upright piano constituted the furniture. We shared the hall with the local boy scout troupe, a sewing group and a singing teacher. I attended Bible study group there with other young folk.

Our meeting consisted of some twenty people, all joined through marriage or business. Dad was connected in trade to most of the men in the assembly. They knew the Church to be self-multiplying, buying up opportunities, doing business in the sea of men and netting gains for God. My father, who now dealt in land, was considering buying the meeting hall, as rumours were circulating of dance classes and the assembly was strongly opposed to this contamination.

The morning after I'd dined at the Townley's everyone was present except Amy Gibbs, at home with a new baby. William sat across from me, near but not next to Mum. Dad sat with Mr Rowe, Mr Buchanan and Mr Gallop. They were our elders. James sat next to me, his young body, with its restless fidgeting, a curious comfort.

I closed my eyes. The Holy Spirit was moving among us. I took James' hand on my left and Mrs Rowe's on my right. James' innocence would hold the Spirit but I doubted that I could conduct it. God would have heard my silence last night, seen the marble encasing my heart. I wondered if James had heard my argument with Mum. Perhaps he would feel sullied having contact with me. I opened my eyes and found my mother looking at me, her eyes the blue of the opal. I quickly closed my eyes again. Mr Rowe spoke forth.

'If the place you go to, brothers and sisters, is a place where everybody does what he likes and all is peace and there is no judgement or dread of God then the place, brothers and sisters, is Luz, not Bethel.'

My cheeks burned. I knew Mum was still staring at me, waiting for me to break down and confess to the assembly. I was not at peace, that much was certain, yet my pillar to God was not yet a pillow of stone. I could still see the angels ascending and descending the staircase. I had nothing to confess.

Our hands still linked, we followed Mr Gallop's lead and began to sing.

My faith has found a resting place
Not in device or creed

89

I trust the Ever Living One
His wounds for me shall plead.

This had long been a favourite of mine. The image of
Christ, bleeding from the hands and feet, violently pierced by
human ignorance, had always given me hope. He had a
capacity for forgiveness that I, one of the ignorant, desperately
needed. On this day, however, the song was not met by any
answering surge of faith inside me.

I must have pressed James' hand with the force of my
thoughts because he pressed back. I wanted to squeeze his
flesh so hard it would burst. What was the matter with me?
I was a faithless girl. Faithless. I wondered what it was like
to go to the pictures.

Mum came over to speak to Mrs Rowe at the close of the
meeting. All around chairs were being scraped back as people
rose to their feet. Bibles were being clasped shut. My mother,
so small and slender, looked a sparrow next to Mrs Rowes'
plump puffin. 'Mr Rowe spoke well today,' she said.

'The Spirit was strong in him.'

'It's a shame Amy could not be here to hear him,' Mum
commented. 'Are she and the baby well?'

'Very well, thank you.' Mrs Rowe, grateful for an audience,
explained in intimate detail her new grandson's feeding and
toilet habits. I watched Mum. Her face was impassive but I
was certain she found this talk vulgar. For her these matters
were to be noticed but not discussed. Mrs Rowe suddenly
nodded towards William's tall figure at the far end of the hall.
'Your William's to be married soon then.'

'They've set the wedding for June. William wishes to save
some more money.'

'He was always a good child.' Mrs Rowe smiled benevo-
lently at me. 'As is this one. Your right hand no doubt.'

Mum regarded me dispassionately. 'This one has a wayward spirit. She always has. But then the Lord equipped us
for responsibility.'

Mrs Rowe's face dropped into folds of sagaciousness. 'Goodness yes, motherhood is demanding.' Her marcasite brooch flashed. 'Daughters are mothers' little helpers though, aren't they?'

Mum's eyes behind her glasses were as fathomless as stones. James had come to stand on the edge of the group. He was half whistling to himself. 'Annie will help me right now,' Mum said. 'We are going home to put the roast on.'

James picked up my hand. It was as if we were back in the circle of prayer, because he squeezed it. 'Can we have rosemary in the lamb?' he asked.

Mum noticed the hands. 'You are really too old to be holding your sister's hand. Do let go now.'

James swung our hands. 'It's the warmth of fellowship.' Mum's lips were thin, but she said nothing.

Mrs Rowe patted him on the head. 'What a good fellow you are. Here's Mr Rowe. We'd best be off.'

Our family moved to the door, in loose formation. Mum led the way, her step sure and her back uncompromising. James and I followed, no longer linked at the fingers, but with shoulders leaning into one another. I felt shy with affection. Dad and William closed ranks in the rear, their steps in time, each with a Bible held firmly at his back.

On the meagre stair outside James and I paused, waiting for Dad and William. The sky was alive with muscular clouds, white masses wrestling each other for space. The thin crown of the gum shivered in the rising wind. I held onto my hat and turned my face into the forceful air. It stung my cheeks and dried my lips but a keen pleasure raced through me. A currawong dipped his wings and soared by on the current, his yellow eye mad and merry. I imagined how James and I could kick our heels and join him, swooping low across the paddock with a fierce grace. My father and William came up behind us and Dad put a hand on James' shoulder. We stood, all four, lifting our heads into the wind like horses. Then I noticed Mum standing by the car some distance away. She was alone, her neat figure a thin upright against the expanse of grass. The wind raced, my father and brothers rode the wind with me. My chest contracted and I went down to join my mother.

Beth visited us at lunch. It was un-Christian I knew, but I found Beth extremely irritating. I thought her easily frightened, and over eager to please. William was very attentive, offering a discreet protection that Beth leant heavily on. She was very fair, with white, white skin, through which the blood ran clearly blue. There was a softness, verging on sponginess, to that skin. It didn't surprise me that Beth was often faintly damp, mopping at herself with crisp white handkerchiefs that she drew from a seemingly inexhaustible supply inside her handbag. I would take Beth outside to feed the goat and in the harsh light I noticed the thickening of my own skin, which had always been somewhat dark. I would stand next to her, in my plain dresses, with my hair plaited and coiled in its usual style and see how she floated against the sky, her pale hair in a loose bun with soft tendrils framing her face, her pale skin merging with the light, her beautiful clothes gleaming and shimmering. I would feel heavy and dour, terribly aware of her delicate movements as she fed the goat. One day I grabbed her hand and plunged it into the bucket of scraps, telling her to take a decent handful. She stood, transfixed, and when I looked at her, her eyes were full of tears. 'If you can't, then you can't,' I said carelessly, and let go her hand. She withdrew it from the bucket and without a word turned and went into the house. I sank my own hand into the unpleasant muck, feeling proud of my sturdiness. Beth was so fragile. Of what use was that?

Beth did not speak a great deal when with us. Yet I would see her in the garden, after lunch, alone with William, and she would be excitedly explaining something to him, her hands describing in graceful arcs the detail she could not fit into words. She would take William's hand, or touch his shirt collar. William would place a hand at her back to guide her, or support her elbow, or simply hold both her hands and look at her while she spoke. I would watch him watching Beth and be weighted by sadness. Later, when Beth would help me prepare afternoon tea, I would be more than ever irritated by her.

Beth did not come to meetings with us. Her family was Church of England. When William first brought her home Mum received her politely but without warmth. That night William spoke to Mum about the visit, over the rabbit stew. This displeased Mum, who said they would speak of the matter later, but William persisted. My brother cut a fine figure of a man, tall and strong and handsome enough to break any woman's heart, including his mother's.

'I want you to understand that I intend to marry E
told Mum.

'She's a nice girl, but she is not suitable.'

'Why ever not? She suits me.'

'Of course. She's pretty, and docile, but marriage is out of the question.'

'Not at all. It's the very question I'll be putting to her.'

Mum's spine did not touch the back of her chair. William was being highly uncooperative, forcing her to spell things out which should not have needed to be spelt out. 'Beth is not of our kind. Have you thought of any children of such a marriage?'

'Yes. Both Beth and I have thought of children. We want to have children.'

Mum looked to Dad for support. 'Walter, speak to your son. Explain why a mixed marriage won't work.'

Dad cleared his throat. 'Your mother has a point. We've both seen what mixed marriages can do, how they can pull families apart. She's a nice girl but there are other nice girls.'

'But she's the only one I want to marry.'

Mum sighed. 'Is Beth prepared to give up the foolishness of her beliefs? Or does she intend to teach your children such things?'

'These are matters for Beth and I to discuss.'

'These are matters for your family to help you with. That's why we're here.'

William's hands lay at rest on the table, his wrists aligned with the edge as we had been taught. 'I would like my family to help me celebrate my happiness.'

'As we will do, when we feel that your decisions will make you happy. This will not make you happy. Any children you have—how are they to learn how to love, honour and obey?'

'Beth and I will teach our children to love, honour and cherish.'

Mum stood up abruptly. She was visibly distressed, and I was very shocked to see her like that. Dad also rose to his feet, but she brushed him away. 'You are being insolent William.'

'I'm not being insolent. I'm going to marry Beth and I ask that you welcome her.'

'You haven't thought this through.'

William also rose to his feet. James and I were now the only ones seated. We both had the look of plucked white chickens, raw and vulnerable. 'I won't bring Beth where she's not welcome, and since we'll be together I won't go where she's not welcome.'

'Don't threaten me William Seeds.'

William's skin was stretched taut across his face. It looked like it could break. 'I'm not threatening you Mum. I'm asking you to be happy for me.'

Mum was a bad colour, sickly, shiny with sweat above her lip. Dad took her hand and she tried to wrestle it away. He held firm. 'We are happy for you son. There are difficulties ahead but we'll work with you to sort them out.'

Mum's wretched face made me want to cry. 'I am not

happy, but I can see that you are obdurate.' She held onto the back of the kitchen chair and her voice was hoarse. 'You are my son and I will not lose you to foolishness. Beth is welcome in this house.'

Beth continued to visit, but she rarely seemed comfortable. James adored her, but this was no surprise as he thought the world of William. I, as I have said, found her irritating, and it is only now that I realise I was jealous. William had always been my protector, and I couldn't stand the claims Beth made on him, which William now sought to formalise. Dad was kind, but Beth suffered greatly under Mum's critical eye. She set the table in a strange manner, she washed the dishes the wrong way, she wasted good potato when peeling, was overly generous with sandwich fillings and her pea shelling was done without attention. The graceful laughing girl whom I could see from the kitchen window, holding onto William, was constrained and awkward when with Mum and me. It suited Mum, and to tell the truth, it suited me. I don't like to admit it, but my jealousy made me mean. I liked seeing Beth diminished.

It was a different matter with Beth's sister Jane. Jane was exceptionally clever and was studying at university. She suffered from deafness in one ear, like me, yet this had not deterred her from her studies. I met Jane rarely, only on those occasions when the two families of the young engaged couple would gather together, yet each time I was acutely conscious that I'd left school at twelve, never to return. Dad had said, after a year of failing grades, that they would keep me at home. In matters of the home I excelled, yet there was Jane, a fellow sufferer, now attending university and doing very well. I didn't like the comparison.

To make matters worse, Jane was no slouch when it came to home skills. It was Jane who cut and stitched Beth's beautiful clothes. I couldn't hope to emulate her skill as a seamstress. Jane was always impeccably turned out and I used to imagine her at university, a glamorous presence amongst the serious young men. She was serious herself, quiet and dark, very different to her sister. When she spoke people attended to her, she treated William as her equal and she met my mother with imperturbability. She frightened me.

We were all on a picnic once, a long way from home, at Kuring-gai. We spread the rug on a bluff overlooking the water, which appeared as a blue chip set in the sandstone cliffs. We'd been squashed together in the car, in the heat, and we were grateful for the sense of limitless space. After walking through the bush and collecting wildflowers—you could do that then, it was entirely the done thing to return from the bush with armfuls of flora—we stretched out on the rug to eat. James perched on the running board.

Jane was seated next to me. I passed her pickles and relish, and the crusty loaf baked fresh that morning. She asked after my training.

'I like it very much,' I replied.

'What will you do when it's finished?'

I looked at her in surprise. I hadn't considered it. To cover my confusion I gave a false little laugh and said, 'There's lots to do at home. I shan't be wanting for work.'

'Have you thought of taking it further?'

'The course only runs for twelve weeks.'

'But there are other courses, and there are hospitals needing staff.'

My hand flew to my ear. 'I couldn't.'

In slow imitation of my instinctive gesture she covered her deaf ear with one hand. 'Why not?'

As if it were a play I left my hand in its protective position. 'You need to take a physical examination. I wouldn't pass it.'

'That makes it difficult, not insuperable.' Her hand still covered her ear.

I didn't recognise the word she used. Suddenly angry I

dropped my hand. 'I don't have your education. I wouldn't be accepted.'

She ignored my sarcasm and lowered her hand. 'You would make a very good nurse. Your education is not what would interest them.'

'That's easy to say when you're at university.' I could hear myself, the petulance and derision, yet I felt driven to speak in this way.

'It has been a struggle for me, even before I started classes,' said Jane. 'It's still a struggle.'

Shamed, I looked away. My mother was watching us and she said, 'Jane, you appear somewhat sallow today. Have you been studying too hard?'

'No Mrs Seeds. I suspect I have a sallow complexion.'

Beth said, 'You have perfect skin Jane.'

Jane leant back on one hand, watching my mother. 'But I look sallow, so I'm told.'

'I think Mum was just concerned that you've been working too hard,' I said.

Jane didn't even bother to acknowledge my comment. 'What would you recommend for this condition Mrs Seeds?'

'But you don't have any condition,' wailed Beth.

'You have misread what I said,' Mum told Jane. 'As Annie said, I was only concerned for your well-being.'

Jane turned to inspect me. It was a flat, clear look, neither critical nor kind. 'The perfect daughter,' was all she said.

William stood up and held out a hand to Beth. 'We're going for a walk.'

'Can I come too?' James leapt to his feet.

My father stirred from his reverie. 'They want to be alone son.'

James was mortified. I stood quickly, breadcrumbs scattering from my skirt. Everyone looked at me, away from James. 'I'll go for a walk with you,' I told him.

Jane produced a book from her handbag and lay down,

resting her weight on one elbow. She could not have more effectively shut herself off from her surroundings if she had erected a wall.

A light wind tossed the tops of the gum trees. James and I watched as the grey-green foliage flipped to reveal its silver underside, and then flipped again to the original colour. It was two trees in one, a piebald, prancing creature.

'It'd be nice to do that, wouldn't it?' James remarked. 'Turn yourself inside out.'

'Two people in one?'

He made a small noise of assent. 'Don't you think we're already two people in one?' he asked, poking the dirt with his toe. 'An inside and an outside person?'

'Maybe,' I said, 'but God can see all of you.'

He turned over a rock and a startled lizard scuttled into the undergrowth. 'It's a shame people aren't more like God, able to see both bits.'

'How can we be like God?' I laughed. 'It's our life's work to seek Him, but we're full of sin.'

'We could try harder,' he said angrily. He ran down the hill, arms outstretched, making aeroplane noises that bounced off the stony cliffs and multiplied in the cavernous silence. He ran faster and faster, as if he were running from something. Maybe from me, I thought. I stood alone, watching the trees glitter and prance, hearing James' engine noises swell and fade. An inside and an outside person. The undergrowth rustled and the leaves danced. I had no idea what was inside me. I was scared to know.

I worked double time on the Monday following the weekend marked by tea at the Townley's. Monday was washing day. Without the luxury of machines washing was an all day affair. Wood needed to be chopped, the copper stoked, soap vigorously rubbed on patches of dirt or sweat, and then, inch by inch, the wet, steaming load needed to be fed into the wringer. Turning the handle on your wringer kept a woman strong in the arms and shoulders, which came in very handy when beating the mixture for cream puffs.

By early afternoon I'd finished the task and I was lathered in sweat and skin lotion. I made up my own formula to combat my dry skin. I ran a bath and carefully washed my hair, massaging some olive oil into my scalp. I wrapped my long wet hank of hair in a towel and dressed in an old frock so that I could sit outside. Mum encountered me in the hallway.

'What are you doing?'

'I'm going outside to dry my hair.'

'At this hour? There's work to be done.'

'I've finished the washing. It's so very hot—I thought I'd wash my hair for class.'

She consulted the bar watch pinned to her chest. 'It's barely one. The washing is not the only work to be done.'

'I'll just dry my hair first.'

'You know that you wash your hair in the morning. This is absolute nonsense doing it at this hour. I want you to take some milk and eggs to Mrs Chapman.'

'I can't go out like this!'

'It's not my fault that you wet your hair in the middle of the day. Mrs Chapman's husband is very ill and she has hungry mouths to feed. Are you saying that your appearance matters more than their hungry bellies?'

I returned to my room and dressed again, putting on street clothes suitable for a visit. I could not go out with wet hair dripping down my back so I plaited and coiled it, stuck a hat on and set out. Mrs Chapman lived a good forty minutes away on foot. The day's heat was at its zenith, with the accumulated ferocity that early afternoon acquires. My shoes kicked up puffs of dust which hung in the air, the particles of dirt too hot to fall straight back to ground. Leaves hung dispiritedly, a matt-grey mass drooping to earth. I shifted the basket on my arm and squinted against the sun. It was unfair of Mum to have sent me out before I'd had a chance to dry my hair. The sun was a yoke across my shoulders and I lowered my head. It really was unfair. I had the right to wash my hair in the middle of the day if I organised my schedule appropriately. I came to a standstill in the hot dusty street. The houses here were spaced well at a distance from one another, but from one house to the next nothing stirred. Not a cow, nor a child, nor a dog, nor a man disturbed the picture. There was only me, kicking up puffs of dust. Only mad dogs, Englishmen and Annie Seeds were out in the midday sun.

I could go home and say to Mum that I was going to dry my hair, and then deliver the milk and eggs to Mrs Chapman on my way to class. I turned to face home. I'd only have to look Mum square in the face and explain to her that this was my plan. I turned again. It was impossible. Mum would not soften. She would probably talk of the hardships endured by missionaries.

I moved forward into the still life. From Mrs Chapman's I could walk a further thirty minutes and catch a tram into Parramatta. I was already dressed for class, except for my wet hair. I didn't have to go home, but could set myself free for the day. My steps quickened and I managed to walk fast enough to ignore the voice in my head that asked how I would explain being absent from home for hours without notice. When had explanation ever helped me? I was better off simply disappearing and taking the consequences later. I was going downhill and I went faster and faster. Thoughts could be left behind.

Mrs Chapman opened the door to me only after repeated knocking. I could hear screaming from inside the house, the piercing cries of children and Mrs Chapman's equally hysterical high-pitched voice turning the space behind the closed door into a danger zone. I stood uncomfortably on the front step, perspiration trickling down my back. Mrs Chapman's face was pinched and the look she gave me hostile. I proffered the basket.

'Mum said you might like some milk and eggs.' I was aiming for a light social tone.

'Did she now Miss Seeds. Isn't that awful nice of your saintly mother.' She did not take the basket.

'They're fresh.'

'Good on the cow and chickens. Isn't that just darn clever of them.'

My bright social face fell off. I could feel it go, as if the glue had melted. 'Mrs Chapman, I'm hot and thirsty and my hair's wet. Could I have a drink of water please?'

Her mouth was still drawn up in contempt but she took the basket. 'You'd better come in.'

I followed her into the house, which was in a state of chaos. There were objects underfoot and scattered down the hallway, which was in sore need of upkeep. Strips of paint curled to the floor, which was uneven. A child, clad only in under-things, hurtled past me and disappeared into one of the rooms. The kitchen was grey and dingy, with more peeling walls. Mrs Chapman took an enamel mug from a cupboard and dipped it into a tin bucket standing in a corner. I shuffled a few steps back towards the safety of a wall, so that I didn't have to loom so obvious in the middle of the room, and my left foot trod on something soft and pulpy. I lifted my foot and saw a dead mouse, in an advanced state of decay, half entangled in the fibres of the rush matting as if woven in. Bits of sodden fur and matter clung to my shoe. Mrs Chapman passed me the glass of water and looked at my foot dangling above the floor. Her face was grim.

'The maid hasn't cleaned this room yet I'm afraid,' she said, hand on hip. 'Good help is so hard to find, don't you think?' I felt assaulted by her stare.

I heard giggling and saw four young children huddled in the doorway, seemingly tumbled one on top of the other like

101

puppies in a basket. They were in various stages of dress, or undress, with slight bodies and pale hair. One of the middle sized ones ran to another doorway and shinned up the wood, feet on either side of the frame, until his head butted the top. He grinned triumphantly at his mother, who said, 'Get down from there you little monkey.' It lacked conviction. The other children giggled and I surreptitiously wiped my foot on the matting. I looked at the mug in my hand, whose water was cloudy. I drank it down in one gulp.

'Mrs Chapman,' I said, 'could I ask a favour?' She looked at me suspiciously. 'Could I sit in your garden to dry my hair?'

'You want my water and my conveniences,' she said sarcastically.

'Please,' I said. 'My mother made me leave the house before I'd dried my hair, and I've a class in town and I can't go with wet hair.'

'That'd be right,' she sniffed, 'your mother's not one to care about other people's feelings.' She looked me up and down. 'She's got you on a string hasn't she?'

I sidestepped for the door. 'I'm sorry. I'll go.'

'No you won't,' she said, 'you'll come outside and sit in the sun. Besides,' she smiled and I saw black spaces where teeth were missing, 'you've got mouse on your shoe and my cup in your hands.'

She took the mug. The children loitered, quiet and intrigued. Mrs Chapman motioned to me to follow her and led me down some sloping stairs to a bare and dusty yard in which a few hens scratched in a half-hearted manner.

'My *garden*,' she announced, with a sweeping gesture, as if showing me Versailles. She disappeared into a lean-to and re-emerged with a towel. She draped this over an upturned horse trough and patted it encouragingly. 'Take all the time you like. If you've got a magic spell for growing things give it a go will you?' I looked past her to where a row of wilted vegetables struggled for survival. The garden bed was ill dug and the soil colourless and hard, with stony debris scattered throughout. Mrs Chapman sighed. 'I don't have the knack, besides not having the time.'

'I could help you,' I surprised myself by saying.

'Not in those clothes you won't.'

'Not today, but later. If you like.'

'Maybe. We'll see.'

She went back inside and I sat down rather gingerly on the towel. I put my handbag next to me and took the hatpins from their nests, laying my hat neatly next to my bag. The children had followed us outside and now started tumbling in the dust. With their thin limbs and scant clothing they did not seem much more substantial than the chickens.

I unpinned and unplaited my hair and spread it across my shoulders. It was still very wet. I found its damp weight unpleasant on my shoulders and tipped my head sideways so that it fell free to one side. With my fingers I gently teased it from my scalp, where it had been glued to my hat, and I funnelled to let the air underneath.

In the sun I grew drowsy. I was staring at a patch of unfamiliar ground with my hair beginning to curl around my face as it dried. I could feel my thoughts evading me, each attempt to think about what I was doing veering off to disappear into nothing. Yet the question was unavoidable. What was I doing here? Where had my sense of propriety gone? The Chapmans were not a good sort of people, although it was only right and proper to help those less fortunate than oneself. But here I was, in Mrs Chapman's yard, in my town clothes, with my hair down. I shook my head from side to side and sat up straight with a quick jerky movement. Maybe I was going mad. How else could I explain this?

Mrs Chapman came down the back stairs with a chipped white mug in each hand. 'Thought you might like a cuppa,' she said. 'Know I would.' She reached over and picked up a strand of my hair. 'You've got lovely hair. It's long, isn't it?'

'I can sit on it,' I said.

'Fancy that.' She took a sip of her tea. 'You never thought to get a bob?'

'It says in the Bible that a woman's hair is her crowning glory. It's not mine to cut.'

'Fancy that,' she said, more faintly.

The tea was strong enough to stand a spoon in. 'Do you believe in God, Mrs Chapman?'

''Course I do,' she replied, quite indignant. 'What do you take me for, a heathen?'

'I just wondered what it would be like to not believe.'

'You're barking up the wrong tree with me.'

'I'm sorry your husband's unwell,' I said. 'I hope he's recovering.'

She was suddenly all sharp around the face again. 'Is that what your mother told you?' She tossed her tea-leaves into the soil nearby. 'My husband's not sick Miss Seeds, he's run out on me.'

'To where?'

'Don't be daft. To Timbuktu or back o' Bourke. I don't know where he's got to.' The face was sharp, I now saw, with pain. I looked over at the children, who hovered like shadows, their playing ceased. 'Don't ask me what's going to happen with them,' she said. 'With us.'

I didn't know what to say. She couldn't even grow vegetables.

Mrs Chapman brushed a hand across her face, knocking away hard thoughts, or fears, or both. 'Your mother's not so bad. At least she sent food. There's some'd not even give me the time of day.' Her mouth soured. 'It's just the way your mother acts sometimes, like she's Lady Bountiful.'

I was mortified to hear my mother spoken of in this way. 'I'm sorry,' I said.

'You came down in the last shower. It's like you've never been outside your front gate. How's that hair? Dry yet?'

I heard the invitation to leave. I put down my mug. My hair was now quite dry. I started to plait it and pin it up. Mrs Chapman watched with interest.

'How you can be bothered,' she commented.

I secured my hat. 'I would like to be bothered with more than my hair,' I said, although I did not tell her, as I had not told Marion, of my desire to save lives. I picked up my mug and passed it to her. 'Thank you for your kindness.'

She shrugged. 'You be grateful you've only your hair to be bothered about.' I did not repeat my thanks.

All the way in to Parramatta I kept thinking of that dismal yard, which had been such a haven for me. At one point I became anxious that Mrs Chapman would tell my mother I had sat there with my hair fanned out to catch the sun. Mum would never forgive me. I calmed, reassuring myself that Mrs Chapman would not say anything. It might not have even seemed strange to her. I, on the other hand, could hardly believe it had happened. I hadn't done anything more odd in my whole life.

Yet I seemed embarked on a strange course. Once in Parramatta I still had some hours before class began. I strolled over to the Roxy, my nonchalance so feigned it was as if I were play-acting myself. I looked vaguely at the posters advertising the latest show. I didn't really know what I was looking for, visible signs of sin I suppose. The posters were intriguing, with their impassioned faces full of longing. Just so had the disciples looked at Christ. Electric light bulbs, now dormant, lined the entrance, but otherwise the building was just a building. I turned away, disappointed, yet also relieved. I could come to this venue. It offered no proof of evil.

I walked down Church Street, peering into shop windows and the faces of passers by. I felt light-headed, as after a fever. I left the main street and a few blocks away came to the

Catholic church on Victoria Road. I stopped so abruptly a man walking behind me slammed into me.

'Geez love, if you're going to have a revelation, do it inside.'

I retreated to the large sign at the corner of the church, advertising mass times. Now this was danger. I could feel it in the quickening of my blood. The Romanists did not allow Christ the Heading of the Church, but put a man in His place, and in their worship of the Virgin Mary, they dishonoured and dethroned Christ. They refused to act on clear Scripture, they were disobedient. They were an apostate church, claiming to be a Christian Church. I knew this.

I ran to class, arriving breathless and hot.

'You were a big hit at home,' Marion told me. 'We think we'll book you for the season.'

'What does that mean?'

'It means we hope you'll come again, silly.'

'I had the best time of my life. I can't thank you enough'.

'That was the best time of your life? We weren't even trying. We're going to the pictures on Saturday night. Want to come?' I hesitated and she added, 'Tom and I are going. Bill might come with his latest flame, but we'll see.'

At home Mum spoke to me while we were doing the dishes. 'Where did you get to this afternoon, Miss?'

'I was at Mrs Chapman's.'

'I told you to deliver milk and eggs, not to stay and natter.'

'She's lonely Mum.'

Mum lifted her hands out of the soapy water and rested them on the edge of the sink. She sighed. 'Annie, remember what the Scriptures tell us, how a church can lose its simplicity in ways that seem innocent at first but which are in fact engineered by the Evil One.'

I twisted the tea towel in my hands. 'Mrs Chapman's loneliness is the work of Satan?' I wasn't clear what the message was here.

'Mrs Chapman's loneliness is a matter between her and

God. Your staying to talk to her, full of the sense of your own kindness, is the doubtful thing.' I twisted the tea towel further. 'You indulged yourself. What seems to have escaped your attention is that you had a job to do, which you turned into something else, and more jobs back home, which you failed to do, and that you had me worried about where you'd got to.'

'I'm sorry.'

Mum resumed washing up. 'That's twice in one week that you've indulged yourself. I think you need to pay careful attention to any temptations you may feel.'

Mum had bared my doubts. I had indulged myself, but not to assuage Mrs Chapman's loneliness. My own perhaps.

As the days passed I vacillated as to whether I should go to the pictures. Simplicity may be lost in ways that seem innocent at first, Mum had said. Was this what was happening to me? By Thursday it seemed merely academic. I made plans to meet Marion outside the cinema.

Saturday brought a balmy summer evening, the light retreating slowly as crowds gathered in knots on street corners. Bright summer colours startled on loose frocks. Girls' heels clattered excitedly, timpani to the bass laughs of boys. I stood just beyond the shelter of the awning, as if poised above a roiling sea. My dress was loosely belted, I wore my single strand of Spanish dance beads, my hair was loosely gathered at my nape and I was hatless. I felt modern, different. After helping Mum prepare for the evening meal I had gone to my room, washed and changed and then left the house without explanation, save a note on my bed saying I had gone for a walk. I had household money in my purse, to pay for the entertainment and the trams. It was clear to me that I was without shame. Looking around at the laughing faces I supposed I was a fallen woman. I didn't seem to care.

Tom was suddenly in front of me, that merry look, just like a currawong, in his eye.

'Been waiting long?' he asked.

'Where's Marion?' I was searching the crowd behind him.

'She couldn't make it. Sends her apologies. I'm afraid you're stuck with me.'

I looked at him and felt suddenly very exposed. He bent forward to peer into my face. 'Cheer up. I'm not bad company.'

I didn't explain that it was not disappointment which he saw but a terrifying mixture of jubilation and anxiety. He held out his arm and I latched on and found my legs were steady enough underneath me, if curiously numb.

Seated in the auditorium I stared at the light fittings, the decorations on the wall and the red velvet curtains. A man was frenetically playing an organ and each tune was met with loud applause. I ran my hand over the plush of the cushions and kept turning my head to look at the noisy crowd, mostly people of our age. The lights dimmed and as the curtain rose Tom picked up my hand and held it on the armrest. The screen was moving and sound was erupting from the front of the cinema and I suspected I was going to throw up.

'Tom,' I said, staring straight ahead, 'I don't think I can concentrate if you hold my hand.'

'Of course you can,' he replied. 'Don't think about it, just watch the screen.'

I tried not to think about it, but the warmth of his flesh was so electrifying that the sensation seemed to blot out everything else. My first impression of the pictures was a blurred mishmash of noise and movement and something akin to nausea. To this day I cannot recall the story of the film we saw that night. I have no idea who the characters were. I have only this memory of Tom like a fall of sheet lightning at my side, and the flickering of the screen. I remember thinking over and over again, as if I were memorising for class, that I understood why everyone referred to the moving pictures as flicks.

The picture eventually stopped, the lights came up and Tom turned to me. 'How was that?'

'I don't know. Was it any good?'

He stood up and pulled me to my feet. 'Don't be so anxious about what I think. What did you think?'

'I honestly don't know. It was different.'

'Fair enough.' He let go my hand and slouched up the aisle ahead of me, fists in pockets.

In the foyer I asked, 'Was it any good?'

'It was no great shakes.'

I was sure he was speaking of the experience of being out with me. He was half-whistling under his breath, looking around, rather like Marion had been the night she invited me home for dinner.

'I'm sorry,' I said. 'I don't know how to be fun company.'

The whistling abruptly ceased. 'We'll make the fun Miss Holy Roller. You just come along for the ride. Come on, I'll walk you to your tram.'

He took my arm and it was like the other night again, me carefree and warmed, alive under a night sky. It didn't occur to me to take Tom literally. I didn't consider that any show, including a show of nobility, needs an audience to appreciate it. I simply thought myself lucky. After all those years of feeling the weight of God's disapproval I was being favoured. Good fortune was gladness of heart, just as I had always imagined it would be.

I lay in bed going over and over the events of the evening, until they blurred and fudged like the play of light on the cinema screen and I was left with a sickly excitement and little to hold onto. Sleep was fragmented and I would half rise to consciousness with my scalp sweating under the weight of my hair, my hands scrabbling to turn the sheets down. Yet when I finally woke, to a still, bright day, I was huddled in a ball, my skin cold and unpleasant to the touch, like that of a skink which has been out of the sunlight. The excitement had turned to an obscure shame and I pulled the sheet and cotton blanket over me for protection.

I pleaded sickness so as not to have to rise and go to the meeting. My mother said nothing, just assessed me quickly with a flat look then left the room, stopping only at the door to say, 'Be grateful your mother can still pray for you.' I curled away. James popped his head round the door to say hello. I was about to tell him I'd been to the pictures the night before but thought it best not to tell anyone. Besides, I didn't want him thinking that it was the films which had made me sick. I longed for William to come into my room and sit on my bed with his puppets but he was away at army camp, where he would stay until he married. I didn't even know if he still had Bob and Scallywag. They might have long since crumbled to dust.

I heard the car doors close and the sound of the engine as it faded up the street. I had not been home alone on a Sunday for many years. I remembered now the particular stillness that descended on the house, the elongation of time. My curtains were moved languidly by imperceptible currents of air and I slowly began to warm as the sun climbed, heating the walls of the house. I wondered if Tom was thinking of me.

I dressed and wandered into the garden. Dad had already started to pull up some of the summer crops and the soil lay turned and exposed, waiting to be planted. I thought of William and Beth, setting up house together, responsible only to themselves and I began spinning, boots scuffing the earth, skirt lifting. Where would we all be when the season turned in twelve months' time? What crops would I plant in my own garden? I stopped spinning. The same. I would plant the same crops as always. Why did I imagine otherwise?

Restless, I searched out seedlings in the workshed, took Dad's good spade and left a note on the kitchen table saying I'd gone for a walk. I set out for Mrs Chapman's, the spade over my shoulder and the seedlings balanced in my left arm.

I remembered how last time I had tramped this road I'd been hatted and high-heeled. Now I was booted and aproned, a regular worker. There was nothing precious or fragile about me, despite what Mrs Chapman thought.

One of the children answered my knock. He stood there, one leg curled up like a pale dirty crane and absently picked his nose while he looked at me. I asked if his mother was home and he nodded. I asked to see her and he trotted off down the corridor. I stood at the door, cradling my spade.

Mrs Chapman was flustered. 'Come to dry your hair again?' she asked, but there was no sting to it.

'I said I'd give you a hand with your garden.'

There was a long pause. 'So you did,' she said, and I heard pleasure under the gruff tone. 'You'd better come out the back then.'

The hard-packed earth and the scratching hens were just as I'd left them. Linen flapped on the clothesline, not exactly white but obviously clean.

'I'll probably have to discard what you've already planted.'

We looked at the dead heads of vegetables wilting on the ground. 'Don't be too hasty now,' Mrs Chapman said, and started to laugh, a sound like a rusty gate-hinge.

I laughed too, leaning on my spade, the at-home sensation I'd remembered from the last visit unfolding inside me.

'Do you need anything?' she asked.

'Water.'

'I've only the tank.'

'It's still water.' We started laughing again, and she nudged me with an elbow.

'You're still water yourself. I'll go make us a cuppa.'

I began to dig, the rhythmic thud of the spade hitting the earth familiar and comforting. It was not good soil, clay bound and littered with rubble. I kept overturning shards of crockery, rusty nails and indistinguishable metal and wooden scraps. I could see that the garden bed had not been properly turned when first dug. In fact, I suspected Mrs Chapman had just made holes and dumped seeds in them. It was a tribute to nature that anything had grown at all. I turned and turned the soil, heartened whenever I saw a worm. They were few and far between. It was hot in the sun and the hard work of driving the spade into the ground, working at it with my boot and steadying the heavy load of soil as I lifted the tool was causing sweat to gather in runnels at my waist and elbows. Peace settled like a benison on my shoulders.

Mrs Chapman joined me with the tea. We sipped at the strong dark brew. 'You can dig all right,' she said approvingly.

'My Dad taught me to garden.'

'I never knew my Dad. He died when I was two.' She heard a noise and looked around. One of her boys was on the roof of the lean-to. 'Don't think I'm going to carry you round if you fall and break a leg,' she shouted. The boy smiled cockily and nonchalantly did a handstand. The lean-to creaked.

'They've no fear at that age,' she said.

'Have you any manure?' I asked, amazed that she was not more concerned.

'No cow, love.'

'What about the chickens?'

'I've never collected it. If you want to scratch around for it we're in the right spot.'

I thought for a moment. 'I don't know how you feel about this, but it'd be good for the garden. Have you any human excrement?'

'Human what?' It dawned on her what I meant, and she cocked her head to one side and looked at me with interest. 'Go on.'

'It's just what the soil needs.'

'Fancy that.'

She led me to an outhouse, which was little more than shaky planks loosely nailed together over a pit. A swarm of flies buzzed over the dark hole and the stench was awful.

We retreated. 'Doesn't the nightman come by?'

'Can't afford to pay him, things being as they are.'

I nodded and took a few more steps back from the smell.

'Tell you what, how about I get the boys to load up some buckets for you.' Mrs Chapman smiled and I saw again the black spaces between her teeth. 'It's their poo after all.'

I accepted gratefully.

The soil was nitrogen rich by the time we'd finished. I'd not brought gloves with me but it was no time for squeamishness, and the nightsoil was well and truly mixed in by spade, so I scooped out hollows for the seedlings with my hands, spacing them at regular intervals as I'd been taught. Then I filled the bucket from the tank and gently trickled water on to the new bed. I repeated this over and over until the soil was moist and dark. I'd been wondering about protection, as the wall of the lean-to provided a sliver of shade only. At least it was in the afternoon, when the need was most urgent. With regular gentle watering I felt the seedlings stood a chance.

'I didn't know such a lot was involved,' Mrs Chapman said.

'Dad always says a gardener needs patience, as well as skill.'

'And not to be scared to get your hands dirty.' She looked meaningfully at mine. 'I'll heat some water for you.'

I filled the bucket again and washed my spade. Mrs Chapman brought me a bowl of warm water and a bar of coarse dark soap, and when I lifted my hands from the bowl she passed me a white linen towel, embroidered in the corners.

'A lady I worked for once, before I married, she gave me that.'

I dried my hands and inspected the stitching. 'It's very fine work.'

'She did it herself.' She took back the crumpled towel. 'I've not used it before today.'

We glanced quickly at one another and then away, shy and pleased. 'She had lovely things, fine lace on her collars and silk for her underthings. When she gave me this towel she said it was for my trousseau. Word had got around that Dick and I were keen.' She snorted. 'A trousseau. This was it.' She smoothed the creases in the damp cloth. 'It was a nice idea but.'

'Did Dick work in the same house?' I asked.

'He was the stablehand. Mad on horses he was. Mad on betting on them too, though his ship never came in.' She picked up the bowl and tossed out its contents. 'Now he's gone and galloped off himself, mad bugger.'

I was soiled and tired and very hungry. By the position of the sun I knew the Sunday dinner at home would have been cooked and eaten. Mrs Chapman had not offered me any sustenance apart from the tea. I felt certain she had none to offer.

I stretched my back. 'I'd best be getting home.'

Mrs Chapman walked me to the front fence, to where the gate hung drunkenly. 'Water every evening. Gently. Don't let the children throw buckets of water on the plants,' I instructed. 'They'll not survive that sort of watering.'

'Don't be a stranger,' she said.

At home I replaced the spade and sat on the back step to take my boots off. I was in my socks, knocking the dirt from the soles of my boots, when Mum came to stand behind the flywire at the top of the stairs.

'Since when have sick girls tramped the countryside?'

'I've been helping Mrs Chapman in her garden.'

There was an ominous silence. Finally Mum said, 'We don't mix with the Chapmans.'

I squinted at her through the mesh. 'She's in terrible need, Mum. I felt I could help.'

Mum pushed the door open and stood over me. 'You could have helped better by coming to the meeting and asking other good folk to pray with you.'

My hair was wild around my face and my apron smeared

with dirt. Mum, even in her housedress and apron, had the look of being freshly laundered and pressed. 'I can't believe a daughter of mine would walk around on a Sunday, the Lord's day, looking the way you do.'

'It was a Christian thing to do.'

'It was a stupid thing to do. You can be a stupid girl.'

I knocked my boot against the step and a clod of mud fell to the ground. My bones were shrinking, my head clouding. 'They're starving, Mum,' I said.

'Good Christian folk are lending a helping hand. You trust your betters and don't be so sure that you know what's best.' She disappeared into the kitchen and only the mesh trembling slightly remained for me to address.

I took my socks off and in bare feet walked to the strawberry patch, the earth cool and silken on my soles. The strawberries were planted next to a grassy flat on which stood the clothesline. I lay down in the grass which was hot and sticky. Couch grass. A line of shade was advancing behind me, flung from the trees which marked the boundary of our property. They were a mixture of trees that I'd helped Dad plant when first we moved to Baulkham Hills. There were two maples in one corner, which in summer provided cool relief and in winter let the low sun warm the back of the house, and then an odd mixture, which sounded as if it wouldn't work, but which in fact did. These trees had been chosen to provide dappled shade rather than deep shade, and paperbarks stood side by side with wattle. In their infancy they'd looked like children from an orphanage, no connecting tissue save for their awkward, ill-matched appearance and their fierce isolation. Dad had been criticised for planting natives, and their knobbly graceless beginnings only confirmed what all our neighbours and brethren already knew—English trees were superior. As they'd grown, however, they'd reached out to embrace each other and their roughened skin and pewtered foliage gave them the appearance of family. They now looked like they should always have been together while the maples looked the unfamiliar cousins, although there was a coherence to the line that included them. It was Dad's gift, for knowing the shape of things to come.

Looking at the peeling bark and knotted trunks made me think of Mrs Chapman, and I turned over in the grass to face the strawberry patch. Heat from the grass was itching through my clothes. I searched the scalloped leaves for the telltale sign of red, and reaching into the bowers I picked three ripe, juicy strawberries. I lay on my back eating them slowly, the flavour made more intense by warmth, the occasional hint of grit a matter of interest rather than concern.

I thought of how Mrs Chapman's yard lacked any shade. In that poor soil, so caked and flattened by neglect and abuse, it was difficult to imagine what could take root deep enough to withstand wind and drought and the feet of children. I rolled over to look at our boundary line once more. Tucked between the paperbarks was another melaleuca, a honeymyrtle, darker of bark and leaf. A sprinkling of creamy blooms decorated the dark green pelt, like icing sugar on a cake. I switched focus to watch an ant laboriously climb to the tip of a blade of grass, only a few inches from my face. The blade dipped, and the ant bobbed delicately, as if preparing to launch itself. Instead it edged closer to the tip and its weight brought the grass blade into contact with another. The ant stepped from one promontory to the next. I lay back, the sky seemingly a hand's-breadth away. I could fold that sky, as I did the washing, tuck it into a clean corner of my cupboard, shake it out on grey days. I thought I'd plant honeymyrtles for Mrs Chapman, funny little trees but sturdy.

James turned twelve during the week and on the following Saturday we had a family dinner to celebrate. William took leave to join us and he brought Beth with him. Mum and I prepared a roast chicken, with trifle for sweets. We sat in the dining room, the linen streaks of white against the gravy-coloured sideboard and chairs.

'How's the nursing going?' William asked me.

'I like it above all things,' I replied.

'Not above *all* things, I hope,' Mum said, frowning at me. 'I would hope God and your family came first.'

My knife slipped on the skin of the chicken and the wing bounced to the other side of my plate. 'It was a figure of speech,' I said, ashamed of my clumsiness.

'You should choose what you say more carefully,' Mum said, picking up the platter of roast vegetables. 'Think before you speak. More potatoes Beth?'

William took me aside after dinner. 'Anything else been going on besides nursing?'

Trying to appear unconcerned I said, 'Oh, I've been out. With a fellow.'

'Good for you. Do you like him then?'

'I like him,' I said, for the pleasure of hearing the words.

'Fair enough. Bring him home when you're ready.'

William's suggestion disturbed me. I realised I'd had no intention of asking Tom or Marion to visit me at home. It was as if they belonged only to the world outside. I couldn't imagine them in this house, across the table from my parents. But to have not considered introducing Tom and Marion to my family showed that I was much taken with clandestine ways. A familiar scooped-out sensation took hold of me. Sickness in my soul. I turned my head sharply and saw Mum watching me from the other side of the room, her sewing held in her lap.

'Feeling unwell?' she asked.

'No. Just tired.'

'You're running things close to the wind, my girl.' I felt my face go stiff at her words. She picked up a thread and snipped it.

I was certain I'd snipped my link to God. The darkness inside me clamoured and insisted. The faces of my family

117

were innocent, pearly in the lamplight. Only in me did the blackness rise like bile.

'What's this?' Dad asked, absently watching Beth and James playing fiddlesticks before the grate.

I saw that Mum was about to speak. 'Dad, where would I find melaleuca saplings?'

Mum snipped another thread. The snap of the scissors was quite distinct.

Dad fingered his moustache. 'I'm not sure any of the nurseries would carry them. What do you want them for?'

'A woman I know needs some shade, fast as possible.'

'A woman indeed.' Mum laid down her sewing. 'She's talking of Mrs Chapman, Walter. Has some notion of making a garden for her.'

James' and Beth's hands stilled. They seemed to be studying the chaos of sticks between them.

'I'll not have a daughter of mine making anything for Mrs Chapman. She can find her own trees.'

'Dad, she doesn't know where to start.'

'She can learn. You're not her gardener.'

'Of course I'm not her gardener. I'm just helping.'

Dad didn't seem to see the difference. 'It's not seemly. I'll not have you going there, do you understand?'

I must have looked mulish, because Mum said, 'You're to do as your father says, Annie.'

There was a loud clatter as James knocked the sticks into a heap. Everybody started. 'Sorry,' he said. 'My hand slipped.' He shrugged at Beth. 'Guess I've lost.'

I left the room quickly. I hadn't responded to either my father or mother. I'd not agreed to anything. As far as I was concerned, I hadn't given my word.

I'll be glad to see Deborah when she returns in the evening.

It's stretching me to look after two babies and I'm very conscious that I've not seen my house since yesterday morning. Hugo, poor confused Hugo, is fretful most of the day and his mood rubs off on Kimberley. Normally she is a remarkably easy baby, but today she is tetchy and at one point, when she and Hugo are both irascible, I could clunk their heads together to keep them quiet. Marla is wonderful, postponing much of her cleaning to give me a hand. When it comes time to leave she is reluctant.

'It's only another couple of hours before Deborah arrives home,' I reassure her, and myself, 'and if I'm lucky, they'll both sleep till then.'

Marla doesn't look reassured. 'Maybe they no sleep.' She gestures to Hugo. 'This one bad sleeper.'

'Then I will sleep the sleep of the just tonight.'

'No worries about that Miss Grace. God happy with you.'

She is sincere and I am deeply touched. 'For a long time I didn't think He was,' I tell her.

'Somebody putting ideas in your head,' she says wisely. 'You good woman. Impossible God no happy.'

I smile at her. 'You're a good woman yourself Marla. I can't thank you enough for your help today.'

She shrugs my thanks away. She waves at Hugo. 'Bye bye monster baby.'

'It's not his fault,' I say.

'No.' She gives Hugo a speculative look. He has his thumb in his mouth and is breathing stertorously through his nose. 'Still, glad he no my baby.' She blows a kiss at Kimberley. 'Bye bye angel baby.' Then she's gone.

Poor Hugo. Already developing a reputation as someone difficult. It's only because he's unwanted. A little lost soul. Yet I have to agree with Marla. I'm glad he's not our baby.

I bend over Kimberley's cot. She is peacefully asleep, no sign now of the peevish spirit with which she's been seized all day. She's all creamy perfection and as I brush a hand

119

lightly over her temple I see the stippled surface of my flesh, so different to her unblemished skin.

I lean down and give her a fairy kiss. 'Age has nothing to do with some things,' I tell her. 'All that anger today. You're as weary as I am.'

I call out to Maggie as I close the garage door to let her know I'm safely home. She waves from behind glass. Inside the air smells stale and I potter around touching objects and opening windows as if I've been away for weeks, rather than overnight. It's not until I've changed into fresh clothes and have the kettle humming on the stove that I feel at home. Settled. There's no doubting the recuperative power of a cup of tea.

Here, in the safety of my home, I can pull Tom Townley out of the shadows and take a good long look at him. But it is Bert's image which crosses the kitchen to greet me, although I note without surprise the broad face and compact body so like Tom's. This house is full of Bert, whereas Tom exists only in my memory. Perhaps it is only in Paddington, that suburb of street performers, that I can retrieve Tom.

Bert and I never went to the pictures, but we travelled. We drove all over New South Wales—I have the photo albums to prove it. Bert had family down in Griffith, which led to the Victorian border, and I had cousins in Lismore, which drew us north. The big adventure was when we decided to look at the opal mines in Lightning Ridge and so headed west. We were full of admiration for the folk who lived underground, it made us think of the Christian martyrs. That was a truly memorable trip, out across the Western Plains and into the blasted landscapes of the big holdings. What made it so extraordinary is that we stayed in motels, and had breakfast delivered to us in the morning on a tray. That tray fascinated me, with paper frills over the glasses, metal lids over the hot food and china so thick you could build with it. After more than fifty years of cooking and serving breakfast it was a very strange feeling, not unpleasant, but strange, to be served a prepared breakfast. Whenever we stayed with family I always helped prepare the meals and lent a hand around the house, but not in Dubbo or Walgett or Lightning Ridge. We hit a kangaroo on that long road north of Walgett, driving as the light dimmed and the animals came to the tarred surface seeking its warmth. Though it was most frightening and revealing—it was the only time I heard Bert swear; he said *damn*, and then repeated, *damn*—it doesn't hold the force in my memory that those breakfasts do.

I never thought to see myself as a lady of leisure, but how else can I describe those days sitting in the car, maps smoothed open on my knee, Bert's hands sure on the wheel, the sun visor angled down a tad to protect my eyes from the glare, but not so much that it interfered with the view? We'd chat a bit, about what was passing before our eyes, and when we'd stop at a park for lunch, or by the side of the road if we were well and truly in the country, we'd spread a rug and I'd unpack a hamper under the sky. Once or twice it rained, and we sat in the car to eat, rubbing away the mist that formed on the glass so we could see out. It was grand, really grand. I never thought to see so much, but it was seeing it with Bert that brought it alive. I've an album of photos, little black and white squares for the first trip, and colour thereafter, recording our wanderings. I learnt more on those trips than I ever did in school. I used to think it a shame that education should be something only from books, when there seemed so much to learn with your eyes and ears and hands. Deborah tells me it was different by the time she went to school, with science expeditions to the bush and jaunts through the real remains of history to improve their minds.

In a wheat field one day, under a moving sky thick with cloud and wind, Bert turned to me and said, not solemn, but serious, 'Let us pray.' I went to bow my head but he told me to lift it high and feast on God's handiwork. While I looked around at the golden earth and the alive sky he said, 'Thank you Lord. Thank you.' Shafts of light fanned the horizon and birds of prey wheeled overhead, their cries sharp and piercing. Connected to God, the landscape and Bert, I said, 'Amen.'

Bert had the gift of preaching, no doubt about it. I've seen him gather in a crowd, as if it was so many drooping stems, grieving for lack of water and support, and tie it up firmly with his words. Lacklustre faces would revive and shine, and I could feel roots take a firmer hold. In those dreadful days of schism in the Church, in the Sixties, when there was so much ill feeling, I'd watch Bert work the crowd like soil, and see how the bitterness and discord leached from the meeting as he spoke. He loved to help things grow. That was his dispensation. When Bert spoke he found a softer God than the one I was used to addressing. Under his guidance I understood that I mattered to the Lord, that I counted for more than a disappointment.

The Sixties were a terrible time for the Brethren, we were a community pulled apart. Billy Graham was the problem, of course, with his refusal to reprove or judge the Pentecostals, Jews, Roman Catholics or Modernists, indeed his open co-operation with them for the sake of gospel. But he can't be held responsible for everything. As a community we chose discord.

Cleave unto thy husband, the Bible instructs, and I did. Bert was a man of love and grace *and* truth, and together we survived the division of the Church. It was Bert's hand on my shoulder in times of trouble allowed me to know that division could be survived.

There's a tap at the back door and when I go to it Maggie stands there, proud and dark. I open the screen door but she won't come in.

'You said you had an appointment, on Friday, with your specialist,' she says abruptly.

'My homeopath,' I correct, 'although he is also a doctor.'

'Is it still all right if I come with you?'

I reach out and take her hand. 'I'll drive you there and back myself.'

She looks past my shoulder. 'It's just that lately, there's this pain.' She gestures towards her stomach, and then her eyes meet mine. 'He's not to know.'

As if I'd tell that husband of hers anything. I'm not sure I'd even pass the Good Word on to him. I squeeze Maggie's hand. 'This is just between you and me,' I reassure her. 'Let me hold onto you, and we'll go and get some tomatoes for your supper.'

She helps me down the ramp. 'Col likes your tomatoes, says they've got good flavour.'

'So they have,' I say. I pick a few, not yet sun-warmed but firm and fleshy. It grieves me that my vegetables go only to his comfort. 'Let me know what *you* think of these,' I say, as I pass her the tomatoes. I look her straight in the eye, a trifle stern. She knows what I mean.

'Do you need a hand back inside?'

'No, I'll potter out here a bit.'

I took tomatoes, fresh from Dad's garden, when next I visited the Townleys. Marion had organised that I meet her in the afternoon, and from her house we would go to play tennis. At least Marion would play tennis and I would watch, having never played tennis in my life. I hoped Tom would also be there. I'd not spoken to him since we had been to the pictures together.

Mrs Townley greeted me at the door, and told me I'd find Marion in her bedroom. I knocked on the door, and entered to find her seated before a dressing-table with wing mirrors, an eyebrow pencil poised above her right eye. She winked theatrically.

'Do come in.' Her voice sounded strange, as if she had something in her mouth. She traced the curve of her eyebrow with the pencil, then sat back to assess her reflection. 'Darling, what do you think?'

'About what?'

'About my eyebrow, darling.' She licked the tip of the pencil and made a small mark just above the left-hand side of her mouth. 'About my beauty spot.' She swivelled to face me and crossed one leg over the other with a swish of skirt. 'I think it rather becomes me.'

I stood there awkwardly. I didn't like the black lines drawn over her eyes and I thought the beauty spot looked silly. 'You don't need make-up. At least I don't think so.'

'You're supposed to tell me I look glamorous,' she said crossly, in her own voice. She turned back to the mirror and brooded at her painted face. 'I want to look like Gloria Swanson.' She saw my bewilderment. 'A movie star,' she explained. She dipped her fingers into a pot of cream and scrubbed the paint from her face. 'Gloria Swanson I ain't.' She didn't say it with any kindness.

At the courts flocks of young men and women clustered around the nets. The rhythmic punch of ball on strings punctuated conversation. Marion made a beeline for one group and as we approached waved her racquet over her head.

'George,' she cried out excitedly. 'Where've you been? The Sudan?'

George, a tall skinny man with close-cropped blond hair, shuffled his feet. 'The what?'

'I thought you'd joined the Foreign Legion. I kept waiting for your letters, isn't that right?' Marion said, turning to me. I'd never seen a comedy act, knew nothing of the role of the straight man. I looked vacant, which was all that was required. Like George, I was trying to make sense of the patter. 'I kept waiting to hear about the flies and the endless dust,' Marion continued, 'the poor rations, the shifty natives and the lonely nights.' She paused for a beat and looked faintly puzzled. 'Why go to the Sudan? That could be Bathurst.'

George rocked back on his heels, shook his head admiringly. 'You're a card Marion. I'm going to the army camp up there next week. You think they'll make a movie of me?'

Marion stepped back and pursed her lips. 'No George. Not even with a costume.'

Everyone fell about laughing. I didn't know what the joke was. I felt as I had at school, tongue-tied and uncomfortable. We moved from group to group, Marion telling funny stories, making amusing observations. I stood to her left, a little behind her, and as a twosome, one alive and witty, the other straight-faced and silent, we entertained each group, one after the other. There was always laughter. Marion's face was pink with pleasure. Years later, watching the Johnny Carson Show with Bert, I saw stand-up comics enact their ritual and I recognised the rhythm. On television the punch lines were marked with two beats of a drum. At the tennis courts the accompaniment was the beat of play as Marion swooped and joked, swirled and laughed. I was full of admiration. I was her foil and I was waiting for Tom.

When he arrived I watched him as he moved from group to group, just like his sister. He would call a greeting, expectant faces would turn, he would speak and be met with laughter. Always laughter. Marion was playing, her skirt flapping as she hurtled from line to net. I was feeling smaller and more insignificant by the moment, waiting to be noticed, fearful that I would be, and fearful that I would not.

'Miss Heavenly Seeds.' Tom executed a small bow. 'Not playing?'

'I don't play.'

'No tennis, no dancing, no flicks, no concerts. What are you allowed to do?'

I didn't like the question. 'I'm here, aren't I?'

He nodded and came to stand by me. We watched the match shoulder to shoulder. Marion did not play well, reaching for the ball too soon, feet raising dust on the court without

125

being sure of their direction. I liked the way she played, eager and unthinking. It was how I would have liked to play myself, if I played at all.

At the close of play we walked back to the Townley's, Marion twirling her racquet in loops and swoons as if it were a dancing partner. She planted herself before us, holding her racquet at arm's length. 'After the ball is over,' she crooned.

'Give it a break Mare,' Tom said.

'What will we do now?' Marion asked.

'I should be getting home,' I said.

'Eat with us,' said Marion.

I looked at Tom. 'Go on, stay,' he said.

So I did.

Marion slouched off to wash and change. Bill was mowing the back lawn and tipped a finger to his temple in greeting. Mrs Townley, flustered as usual, was plucking a chicken over the laundry tub, her nose screwed up, the bird pale and slippery in her hands. She greeted us and wrestled a feather loose. She was plucking against the sweep of the feathers.

Tom leant towards her and sniffed. 'Chicken madeira? Or chicken in sherry?'

Mrs Townley patted her hair with the back of her hand. 'I haven't started cooking yet.'

'I think you have. I think you're well and truly cooking.' Tom stepped into the laundry and picked up a glass standing on the shelf above his mother. It was full of pale gold liquid.

'Put that down,' Mrs Townley said, very red in the face.

'And then you'll put it down.' He set the glass back on the shelf. 'You're making hard work of that chicken as it is.'

'Can I help you?' I asked. Mrs Townley lifted her chin and looked down her nose at me. Very much surprised, I elaborated. 'With the chicken.'

'I don't need any help, thank you.' She'd never been so proper with me. I didn't know why I'd offended her.

'We could argue about that, couldn't we?' Tom said. 'A tumbler-full. It's not even five o'clock.'

'You watch your tongue. You eat the food I cook, you wear the clothes I wash. Don't criticise me.'

Tom stepped back, hands up as if fending off untruths. 'Mum, Mum, don't get on your high horse now. I'm not criticising you. I'm just interested in your habits.' He slung an arm around my shoulders. 'Why, as Annie knows, we're one big happy family.'

I smiled uncertainly. They were a happy family. 'Take Annie inside,' Mrs Townley said, cheeks still very red. She really did not have the knack of plucking. 'Offer her a cup of tea or something.'

'Or something?' Mrs Townley looked like she might cry. Tom lifted his arm off my shoulder. 'I'll see what I can do.'

He held the door open for me. 'Are you sure I can't help?' I asked. 'I don't think your mother likes that job.'

Tom motioned for me to continue into the hall. 'You're amazing,' he said. 'Do you want a sherry?'

'No, I don't drink.'

'Never had a sherry?' I shook my head. 'What do you use for communion?'

'We don't have communion, not with bread and wine at any rate. We hold hands.'

'That's quaint.' We had arrived in the living room, dark with furniture, heavy with antimacassars. The curtains hung like gloom. Tom sat down on the piano stool and patted his knee. 'Come here.' I sat, gingerly, looking straight ahead. Tom jiggled his knee. I jiggled with it. He cleared his throat. 'Miss Holy Roller. Are you with me?'

I turned to look at him. Our faces were very close. I could see the pores of his skin, even in the dim light. He had a faint shadow on his chin. He put a hand behind my head and bent me down. When he kissed me I was conscious of my stiff

127

neck and my hands squashed in my lap. I was conscious of his mouth, which wasn't mine.

He pulled back. 'Put your arms around me,' he said. I did, and when he kissed me again my breasts were mashed against his chest. I felt something soft and pulpy in my mouth. It was his tongue. I pulled back almost violently. 'You don't like that,' he commented, neutral.

Marion called my name. It sounded like she was in the kitchen. I stood up. 'Don't get upset now,' said Tom, standing up next to me. 'You don't know enough to get upset.' He ran his hand down my back and I shivered. 'Come on, we'll find my lovely sister.'

At home Mum looked at me as if I were a cockroach. At breakfast there was no food for me, and when I sat at the table Mum stood up. When I stood to prepare myself some food, Mum resumed her seat. After breakfast Dad read the Bible while we prepared for the meeting and James rummaged in the garden, searching for beetles which he examined in the sunlight, his lips moving soundlessly at the revelation of their iridescent colours.

It wasn't that Dad and James weren't speaking to me, more that they had withdrawn from the arena, leaving the space to Mum and me. They had detached themselves from the tension, leaving it to bind Mum and I together. I felt very lonely, deeply afraid and defiant as any striking worker. I wasn't convinced that I was doing the right thing, but I felt compelled to this course of action. I just wished I could cosy up to Dad or James, to temporarily escape the loneliness. When Mum looked at me with contempt, some part of me wanted to reach out my arms, calling her name over and over again, to be reassured that I was her daughter. I wanted her to tell me that she loved me, that she understood why I was behaving the way I was.

Instead, I sought to become an outcast. On Monday I washed and on Tuesday I polished all the wooden furniture in the house, beat all the rugs, dusted all the skirting boards and picture rails, and ironed the pile of freshly laundered linen, beads of sweat decorating my lip. I loved the odour of hot damp cotton turning to dry warmth, this side of scorching, but with that more acrid odour lingering in the background, as if waiting for a cue to enter. I loved nosing the heavy iron down the length of a sheet, watching the wrinkles smooth and the grain in the cloth settle in one direction, like fur on an animal after stroking. I'd starched all the sheets and table linen, and their semi-stiffness added to the pleasure of smoothing their nap. Tablecloths, serviettes and sheets snapped satisfyingly as I folded them once they had aired.

On Wednesday I moved from tub to sink, cleaning enamelled sufaces with bicarbonate of soda and vinegar. And without a word to my mother I washed, dressed for class and left the house early, drawn to explore as if the Lord Himself was pulling the string.

I got off the tram in Parramatta and watched as it bucketed towards the river. I crossed the road to stand momentarily in the shelter of a clump of crepe myrtles, and then I started up the street, turned the corner, walked for a block, made another turn away from the river and arrived at my destination. It was the Roman Catholic church. I licked my lips, very dry in the mouth. Dared I go in? This truly was fellowship with unbelievers. The Anglicans were one thing, from a lukewarm, spurious church, but the Roman Catholics were infidels. The hairs rose on my arms, but I entered.

Inside the church the air was cool and dry. I had expected damp. There was no sign of people, although an expectant hum filled my ears. This was a bigger church than St John's; there was a greater expanse of pew and carpet, a longer shell of brick, a higher arch of plaster and beam. Great chunks of coloured light lay over wood and brick. If I stared at these patterns long enough it was easy to believe that the colour had fallen from the glass, tumbled to earth as if pushed from behind. Angels of light, hurtling through space, streaming from above to take insensate, transparent, lovely form on earth. If I looked up I would see bleached glass, colourless and blind. I looked up and the jewelled colours remained aloft, endlessly refracting their richness with impartial generosity. The stained glass had no concept of hoarding its treasure. It was wealth for all.

I sat in a pew at the back of the church. I saw small altars in side pockets of the church adorned with thin candles, some of which were alight and many which were not. Pedestals jutted out above head height down the length of the walls, and on these stood painted images. I looked closely and saw with horror that some were graven images of Christ. The others I did not recognise, except for the young woman with a blue robe falling from her shoulders, with her hands held out, whether in supplication or comfort I wasn't sure. She, I knew, was the Mary raised by Roman Catholics to idolatry. I stared at her waxy colours, her moonstruck face, and fascinated, stared some more until I realised I was imagining myself poised high above the heads of the congregation, blue robe swirling to my feet, faces turned worshipfully toward me. My heart knocked audibly in my ears and I looked away. No wonder the Church was held in such disrepute. What spells were cast here to invoke such thoughts?

A door opened in a cupboard stuck against a wall and a man in a long black gown stepped out. Florid faced, with bushy grey hair and spectacles slung around his neck, he saw me sitting at the back of the church and I saw him straighten his shoulders. He gestured toward the cupboard. I stared at him, aghast. His hands dropped to his sides and indecision rippled his gown. He fumbled for his glasses, perched them on his nose and, peering at me, once more intently gestured toward the cupboard.

I had never been more frightened in my life. I stood, knocking my knee against the prayer rail, and backed away from him until I reached the exit, where I turned and ran. I sprinted down the stairs, up the street, across the road, and when I reached the middle of the next block I slowed to listen to my own breathing.

For what purpose had that black-frocked man tried to inveigle me into a cupboard? I had been in the den of Satan and, more to the point, I had willingly placed myself there. I leant against a fence to support myself, and when I closed my eyes the blue-robed Mary opened her mouth wide, laughter pouring forth like bitter flames to scorch me. Her robe lifted to reveal black wings and she launched herself from her pedestal, taloned fingers reaching for me. I opened my eyes and sky, pavement, suburban street swung dizzyingly before me. Clutching the fence post I fought back tears. I longed for my mother, for her flat statements about the insidious work of the Devil, and the need to resist.

At class Marion gave me a doubtful frown. 'You look like you've seen a ghost.'

'I probably hurried too much to get here.'

'Your mum should leave you more time to get ready. She makes you work too hard.'

Fury rose in me. 'My mum's just fine. Leave her alone.'

Marion went red. 'No need to snap at me.' She turned away and we worked alongside each other, without speaking, until Marion said, 'Look, sorry. I was just standing up for you.'

I looked at her coldly. 'You're always having a go at my mother.'

Marion banged a kidney dish on the table and I saw the instructor look our way. 'You're always telling me things about her.'

I folded my lips in prim disdain. My straight back told her what I thought of her. Marion leant across and whispered, 'Damn you.'

Shocked, I stared, and she stuck her tongue out at me, but I didn't take any notice, I was too occupied with the black angel in the blue robe, the fallen angel turned to evil, shrieking at me as it flew across the room to gouge my eyes.

I had fainted, it seemed. The nursing class panicked, much to the instructor's chagrin. While the students twittered, the instructor, so I was later told, lay me straight with my arms by my side and my collar loosened, checked my head to see if I had caused damage during the fall and felt my pulse. Marion meanwhile telephoned her mother. Her family was at home, it being early evening, and Mr Townley sent Tom in the car to take me home. By the time he arrived I was sitting in a chair, rigid with humiliation. Marion sat next to me but we did not speak.

I couldn't meet Tom's eye as he shepherded us to the car. I wanted to sit in the back but Marion and Tom were insistent that I sit in the front. Street lights flickered on as we drove through Parramatta.

'What was all that about?' Marion's voice was muted by the engine.

'Nothing,' I replied.

'Come on,' she said, testiness a thin disguise for hurt. 'You came to class in a terrible mood, you were mean to me, then you fainted.'

I said nothing and the seams in the road clicked under the wheels like railroad tracks.

'What's happening?' Marion asked.

'Give it a break,' Tom remonstrated.

There was silence and then Tom asked, 'You feeling better?'

'I'm fine thanks.'

'You don't seem fine.'

'Give it a break Tom,' came the caustic comment from the back seat.

I pointed out my street and as the car came to a standstill I fumbled for the door latch. Tom was out of the car before I had the chance to tell him to stay put.

Marion leant out the window. 'See you tomorrow then?' she asked.

I nodded, but I didn't believe that I would ever go to class again. As I walked up the front path a movement in the shrubbery, in an oily patch of darkness, heralded the return of the black angel. I shivered uncontrollably and putting out my hand for support touched Tom. We stood still, me clutching his jacket, him looking down at me. I could hear voices whispering in the dark, the word slut echoed in my head. I groaned.

'You're in a bad way,' said Tom.

'You're full of sin,' I hissed at him. I let go his jacket and my hand stayed crumpled in a fist, hanging as if disembodied in the air between us.

'You're probably right,' he agreed, 'but I think it's your own you're more worried about.' I drew in air between my teeth, a slow noise like gas escaping. 'So you kissed me,' he said. 'You going to have a fit about it now?'

'You kissed me.'

Tom leant down. 'Miss Pure As The Driven Snow, you were there.'

I knocked past him, eyes averted as at a catastrophe. I fell over the top step and crashed to my knees, my handbag bouncing away to lie like a foreign object on the boards under the porch light. Malevolence was in the air.

Tom bent to help me up. I struck his hand away. 'Don't touch me,' I cried.

'For Christ's sake.' He straightened. 'You're going on like this because of a kiss? I should have gone the whole hog.'

There was the creak of a car door opening. Marion called out, 'You two all right there?'

I lay sprawled on the stairs. As I struggled to my feet Tom called out to Marion, 'She's having some kind of fit.'

The front door opened and Mum, small and spare, stood

framed before us. Tom was visibly relieved. 'Mrs Seeds,' he began.

'Do I know you young man?'

'No, that is I—'

'Then I'll thank you not to stand in my front yard shouting lies to the world.'

Tom looked at Mum, his mouth open, and then he half laughed. Shaking his head he said, 'Your daughter Mrs Seeds—'

'I'll take care of my daughter.'

Mum took my hand in a painfully strong grip. I was in the shelter of the porch now, and I bent down to pick up my handbag. The light hurt my eyes.

Tom made that sound again, as if he was about to laugh. 'Thanks for bringing my daughter home Mr Townley,' he said, to no one in particular.

'Looking at the condition of my daughter I don't think I need to thank you for anything.'

She pulled me inside and firmly shut the door. I had a glimpse of Tom, disbelief and anger warring on his face. I did not acknowledge him.

The bone in my wrist was aching from the pressure of Mum's grip. The house was breathing quietly, expectant, curious. I knew this house intimately, knew every corner where skirting boards met and cobwebs formed, knew every angle of fireplace and hearth, knew every catch of cupboard door and window sash. I'd cleaned this house from floor to ceiling, from wall to wall, had assiduously removed dirt and dust from every surface, no matter the shape or size. Yet I knew this house to have spaces, invisible to the eye, that could not be reached, pockets that shaped themselves to disappearances. Dad and James had tunnelled into hiding, but here on centre stage I faced Mum. The house was witness.

'Can you explain yourself?' Mum asked.

'I fainted in class.'

Mum pressed harder on my wrist. My sturdy bones were as chicken wing tips in those slender hands. 'This blackness in you. It is my curse.'

My mouth opened in a soundless *oh*. With unerring certainty Mum had put her finger on the trouble. It was impossible to hide from her, as it had ever been.

'I have battled with this sickness in you all my life,' she said. 'You have been my constant burden.' Her voice rose. 'God has always tested me with you.'

I was shaking, Mum's fingers around my wrist the only solidity. 'I went to a Roman Catholic church,' I confessed.

'Why have you done this to me?' she asked.

'I wanted to know what was out there.'

Mum let go of my wrist. 'It's not about what's out there. It's about what's in here.' She touched my chest, my head. 'Why did you think you had to look somewhere else?'

I shook my head, mute. Mum put her hand on my shoulder and ordered me to kneel. I did, and she joined me, our hands steepled and our heads bent, our bodies a guard of honour in the hallway. 'Lord, see my child, your child, born to the knowledge of sin. In her the sin has multiplied, a malignant growth. Help me to cleanse her.'

My heart opened in mortification to the Lord. 'Forgive me,' I cried. To Mum. To God.

A long and painful silence followed. My kneecaps had that smashed feeling that comes from kneeling too long. Mum said, 'I don't believe that forgiveness is yours just for the asking.'

Cold fear compressed me. I could smell it. 'Do you think I've not been heard?'

'I'm sure you've been heard. But God is listening to your intentions, not just your words.' She got to her feet. 'Go to bed. Think about this. I don't think saying forgive me is all that's required.'

The spareness of my bedroom greeted me, like a familiar

face. This room was home. What lay beyond was the world. The apostle John had said, *We know that we are of God, and the whole world lieth in wickedness.* In Bible study had I not announced, finger trailing the page for wisdom, voice firm in my offering to the Lord, 'There are two great spiritual inter-heavenly systems. There is the Kingdom of God, and there are the Kingdoms of the World'? Mrs Gallop had encouraged me. 'What does that mean Annie?' I had been proud with my answer.

'God is related to the Church, whereas the world is related with the Devil and the flesh.'

When Tom had put his tongue into my mouth, snaking inside me with flesh and saliva, what further proof had I needed that I was being entered by the Devil? In the mirror I could see my nipples, clearly defined under the stuff of my dress. My hand travelled across my breast, feeling its plump weight, moved down across my belly, curving towards the part of me for which I had no name. In the glass I looked glittery and wide-eyed. The apostle James had said, *Know ye not that the friendship of the world is enmity with God?* Mrs Gallop's question, directed to the group at large, had been an easy one: 'Can a Christian have fellowship with the world?' I had leant forward and replied, 'No, a thousand times no.' Mrs Gallop had smiled, the moles hillocking her cheek peaking with approbation.

In the glass I looked depraved. Too much of me was flesh. Warmth in my body, Marion clicking her heels, Tom looking at me with speculation, happiness rising in me, soft as dough. Too much of me curving towards the sensations of flesh. A tongue in my mouth that was not mine, my hand touching my body to stir me to bestiality, Marion's crimson smeared lips, Tom flying across the room toward me, blue robe turning to black. I slid to the floor, my hands writhing away from my body to keep me clean. When is the world not the world? It is always the world, especially when it sparkles and seems innocent and nice.

At breakfast Dad spoke of building a cottage at Dee Why. We had motored up the peninsula twice, winding along the hilly tracks to stay in rented accomodation and feel sand between our toes. Returning home from these holidays we'd found it difficult to leave the rasping surf, the long walks which stretched calf muscles, and the gritty surfaces which belonged to the toss of wind and wave. Mum would cluck her tongue, endlessly wiping down benches and breadboards, but James and I would laugh at the sand in the jam and the sticky saltspray on cups and plates. I loved being able to ruck up my dress, put on my boots and go marching down the beach, watching the Lord at play. When James and I dared waves, running up and down the sand, loud as seagulls, we were at play too, and I felt at one with God. It was a feeling I prized and held onto, as others treasured rocks or shells or vials of sand brought back to dry-hilled suburbs at the end of the vacation.

James, excited by Dad's proposal, began to plan his next summer holiday. He was undeterred by the fact that the cottage had not yet been built. He spoke of inviting a friend from school to stay with us, and thought they would probably climb the cliff at Long Reef, and gather marine specimens on the rock platform that spread at the base of the cliff, a ruffle to its height. Animated, he sketched visions of shared solemn discovery against a limitless sky and sea, birds the sole witness to two boys watching sea anemones pulse open and close, the timing that of a heartbeat.

Mum and Dad looked at each other over his head. 'I don't think we'll be inviting anyone else to stay,' Dad said. 'This will be for family only.'

James shed his animation. It fell in dry husks around him. 'I just thought,' he said, 'someone to play with.'

'Your family will be there,' Mum said. 'We don't need outsiders to make us happy.'

Dad patted my hand. My amazement at this held his question in suspension. By the time gravity had hooked it into me I wasn't sure if it wasn't a statement, after all. 'We don't need outsiders to make us happy, eh Annie?'

Across the table James was chewing his lip. His eyes entreated. He looked like a dog. You could hit a dog and he'd hunker down and look at you just like that. Dogs could be pathetic.

Mum and Dad were leaning into me, benign attention. William had gone, but here we were, a family still. 'We don't need outsiders,' I flatly agreed. James' eyes muddied and he pulled in behind his skin. I was safely tucked behind mine, and happy for James. He no longer had the look of a trusting hound. He couldn't go around looking like that. He was liable to get hurt.

'What fun we'll have,' said Mum.

James and I sat silent, imagining sea anemones, their sticky red mouths closing in the blank stillness.

We moved through the house as if swimming slowly underwater. Emerging from the interior gloom, at first indistinctly, then taking familiar shape, James would plane toward me. We would exchange muted glances of recognition, constrained gestures of greeting. We didn't speak. The air was encrusted with our unspoken thoughts; we would paddle away from each other. I would not let myself recall that James was only twelve. That I was only twenty.

Elsewhere Mum was attentive. I was reminded of being sick as a child, of her cool ministrations that had brought relief to my fever-ridden condition. One day I found myself standing in front of my mirror, the sampler a riband pressing down on my reflection. *Be sure your sins will find you out.* I raised my hand to my forehead, testing for fever. I was surprisingly gelid. Behind me I saw my mother rise from where she had knelt to press her hand to my brow as I stared up at her from my sweat-soaked sheets. I had pleased her. The fever had broken. I turned, as if I would catch us both still there, forever held in that moment of intimacy, me a bleached wan child, Mum a handsome young woman. But we were held only in memory. I turned back to the mirror. I was not a handsome young woman. How could I have imagined that Tom Townley had kissed me for any reason other than malice?

Marion called by. I heard her footsteps on the path, leaping to the door. I drew back into the embrace of heavy curtains and linen protectors, the dead weight of objects. Mum answered the door. I couldn't hear what was said, only the scrape of voices, the insistent note in Marion's voice, the barred note in Mum's. Marion departed, the house set against her back. Mum found me standing like a forgotten item in the middle of the room, duster hanging limply. She spoke sharply and I stirred; resumed my slow progress through dust and time.

On Sunday we drove to the meeting. It was the first time I'd been outside the house since the night I had fainted. I'd not even been in the garden, to water or hang clothes on the line. By unspoken agreement Mum had taken on all the tasks to do with the outside. The shroud of the house had become my second skin.

The clarity with which I registered the passing scenery, the pulsing light thrown over the world and its sharp edges again reminded me of my childhood illness. This was how I'd seen the world on the drive to the doctor's after months at home. I remembered. The familiarity of vision thrummed in my blood, a surge of recognition, a prayer perhaps, or a confession. After the descent into darkness, and the repulsion of evil, came clarity. Twice now God had vouchsafed this knowledge. I nursed it carefully.

This tender certitude was a gift I brought to the meeting. Not to be spoken of, but proffered in spirit. The four of us sat apart, Dad with the elders, Mum directly opposite me, James tucked away to my right where I couldn't see him. We sang, we prayed, I merged with my fellows in the eye of God. Then Mum rose to her feet, neat figure livid with righteousness, and words spattered from her as she stared at me, pointed to me. *Defiler, wickedness, enemy of the Holy Spirit, flesh and the Devil.* The words smashed at me, a current swirling all in its force. My neighbours swayed in their seats. *Christian charity requires that we testify against a sinner for her own sake.* My brethren leant forward to stare and taste blood. *To help her understand her position.* A rustle of approval shook the circle. My mother reviled me, the blue of her eyes pinning me to her truth. My fellows quivered with approbation. The temperature rose. My father sat staring at his hands in his lap, Mrs Rowe's tongue repeatedly flicked the corner of her mouth, sweat gathered above my neighbour's lip. Words were unleashing bolts of energy, the circle murmured and shone and in my mother's eye I saw that there was no redemption.

And now I'm on the verandah, in the cool green gloom. I'm angry, angrier than I've ever been in my life. I'm burning with rage. I take a glass of water, I put ice in this glass of water. But the ice won't fit, it's a troublesome piece of ice. I'll make it fit. I chip away at that ice, splinters fly off in different directions. They'll melt to nothing. No matter. I can make it fit. Now I'm cooling down, cooling off, rage hissing out of me like steam. I smash another piece of ice, jam it into the glass, make it fit. It can't resist me. It starts to melt. I'm getting cooler. If I hold the glass against my face the skin goes numb. If I hold the ice in my mouth my mouth goes numb. Everything numb. I pick up my embroidery. I prick my finger and my blood seeps into the white cloth, staining and spreading. No matter. I can wash it out: I can bleach it, leach it, make it white, make it pristine, make it pure. There'll be no blood staining my linen. No blood at all. I'm cool now, the green gloom surrounds me, it makes it hard to see. The bead of blood on my finger hardens. No need to think. No need to feel. I'm cool. It's dark. I can wash my blood. I can clean things up. I can sit, pious and stupid.

I sit.

'Did you know Grandma had a sister locked up in an asylum?' Deborah asks. Kimberley is kicking up and down in her bouncer, talking excitedly to herself.

'I knew Jane.'

'Did you?' Deborah sits forward. 'What happened?'

'I've never been sure. But an asylum was no place for a woman like Jane.'

'So she wasn't mad.'

'I don't know what happened. William was already married to your grandmother. Jane and I had been bridesmaids. In fact she made the dresses, they were exquisite.'

Deborah is very interested. 'What was she like?'

'Clever, very clever, and dark. Pretty, though not as pretty as your grandmother.' A small whirlwind shakes me and unexpectedly my eyes fill with tears. 'I don't know what happened to her.'

Deborah looks mortified. 'Aunty, I'm sorry.'

I pull a handkerchief from my sleeve. 'I should know, don't you see? Why don't I know?'

'Probably everyone was very tight-lipped. I didn't know till I was twenty-five. And Mum didn't find out till she was thirty or something. I mean, it was the proverbial family skeleton.'

I blow my nose. 'But I was there. I knew Jane. I should have asked.'

Deborah sits back and gives me a very direct look. 'Fair enough. Why didn't you?' Faced with that even question I suddenly see why she is so good at business.

I wasn't going to come out of this in any sort of good light. 'It was easier to not ask any questions, to just accept the news that she'd become disturbed and needed protection. It was easier because I didn't have to know how frightened I was, and,' this is really most difficult, 'because I could feel smug and superior. I'd always been in awe of her you see, she was so certain. I think I felt like she'd got her just desserts.'

Deborah doesn't shy away in horror. 'Poor you,' is all she says.

Kimberley bounces and in the long silence the creak of springs and her heels hitting the floor are the only sounds. The baby chatter has ceased. I sit very still and what I know is not so hard to find. 'She'd been to university, was the first woman accountant in the state. She set up shop for herself.' I tuck my handkerchief away. 'They said it was because she was jilted, but I don't think it was that. Or not only that. She was still living at home, and she got angry, probably about everything. Chopped up all her dresses and the curtains and the bedclothes one night with a pair of scissors. Yelled at her mother. Maybe tried to hit her—I'm not sure. So they locked her up, for her own protection they said. They thought she'd hurt herself.'

Deborah sighs. 'Or stay angry.'

'She had every reason to be angry. We all despised her cleverness. Thought more of her dressmaking—no wonder she chopped up all those dresses. When she was jilted everyone nodded wisely, as if it was only to be expected.' Across from me Deborah is intent and quiet. 'She must have been very lonely.' On Deborah's face I see neither judgement nor disdain—she remains attentive. 'When I asked after her I was always so, so lofty.'

'I've seen you lofty. It's not a pretty sight.' She is teasing me, being gentle. She takes Kimberley out of the bouncer onto her lap. 'Did you know that Grandma visited her sister every week until Jane died?' I shake my head. 'What I find amazing is how she could do that, every week, year in year out, and keep it from her family.'

I think of Beth, that timid, pretty girl gone to fat, the nervous complaints and dependence on William. 'That took a lot of courage.'

Kimberley is now bouncing herself on Deborah's lap, sausage legs thumping up and down while she grunts with satisfaction. Deborah holds her firmly under the arms. 'I thought maybe Grandma was worried she'd go mad herself. It certainly explains why she was always so suspicious of intelligence. She must have thought the two went hand in hand.'

'She adored Jane, thought the world of her.'

Deborah laughs. 'The first time she met Peter she took him aside and said, *She's very clever you know*, and Peter nodded and said he knew that. She looked at him seriously and then let him go and the poor guy didn't have a clue what it had all meant. It was a warning, can you believe it?'

'Of which he took no notice,' I remind her.

'Only because he didn't know it was a warning.' She buries her face in Kimberley's hair and runs kisses over her scalp. 'We wouldn't have you angel face, if he'd taken any notice.'

'Or if you had.'

Watering my roses that evening I think of Beth. I was always very lofty with her, and Deborah's right, it's not a pretty sight, not in life and not in memory. I wave to Mrs Maguire across the street who's also got the hose out. To her credit she waves back. I fling the hose around to watch beads of water arc and fall. Thirty years ago I tried to convert her, and was over there every other day with tracts and homilies about procreation. I was particularly concerned about the latter, the Maguires being Roman Catholic and her progeny numbering six. It got to the point where, as she saw me crossing the street, lecture forming on my lips, charitable condescension discernible in the set of my shoulders, Mrs

Maguire would hurriedly exit the house, shopping basket on her arm. 'Just got to pop up to the shops,' she'd call out, in an attempt to halt my battleship approach.

'I shan't be long,' I'd call back, waving my fistful of tract, 'I've just got some reading material for you.'

'Got to run,' she'd say, backing away, desperation leaking out under the gay neighbourliness, 'or I'll miss the butcher's specials.' And she'd be off, legs working like an Olympic sprinter to carry her away. I console myself now with the thought that Mrs Maguire's health improved at that time, she was taking so much physical exercise. She grew quite trim.

When I think of myself during that time I shudder. For the first ten years after William married and moved out there were the four of us at Baulkham Hills, Mum, Dad, James and me. I didn't leave the house much during that time. Then James died, and the three of us watched him die, watched that slow wasting of youth and promise. I had most of the nursing responsibility and based it on what I'd learnt from my mother rather than on what I'd learnt in class. I refused all connection with what had been offered to me. And couldn't see that I offered nothing to James.

We moved him to the cottage at Dee Why, hoping the sea air would bring relief to his tortured lungs. But still he suffered from the terrible humidity. Then Mum, James and I rented a house at Leura, in the mountains, while Dad stayed in Parramatta to run the business. He'd join us on weekends and we'd go for short walks in the bush, all four of us. It was all James could manage. After a while he couldn't even manage that.

It wasn't a question of sin with James, his imprisonment by illness. Innocence had always shone from him, he brought joy to everyone who knew him. Mum was in despair, knowing that her prayers were not to beat back evil but to ask for a gift from God. She well understood why God would call James to Him at an early age, why He would want that innocence to shine in life everlasting. She felt hopeless in the face of his ill health and was glad to leave the nursing to me.

When I think of myself at that time I shudder. I should shudder. My brother faded, unable to hold onto life, convinced that it offered him nothing. Nothing that he wanted. I aided that conviction, having given up on the possibilities that came my way, having chosen something restricted, something stupid and narrow. The hose is angled to the ground, a muddy puddle spreads at my feet. I slosh across the wet grass to the tap, and turn the water off. Memory can be a cruel and lonely thing. This knowledge has been beating in my blood for years, but I've been too much of a coward to face it. I step around to the side of the house, to where I am hidden by bushes, and lean against the cold bricks. I hold responsibility for James' early death. What hope could grow in him when he saw me extinguish it? I beat my fist against the bricks and feel the old flesh tear. James, James, I am so sorry. You had a terrible coward for a sister. I loved you so and I took your hand and said this way, come dearest, this way, and this way was a dead end. I survived, like a stone-age fish inextinguishable in mud while the fresh water renews its passage overhead, but you stopped breathing. Didn't want to live with your eyes and ears all stoppered up like me. Didn't see it as a life.

I did. I nursed you to death, never once asking you what you felt about dying, or why you were dying. Read from the Bible to you—endlessly. I remember once you put out a hand while I was reading, you struggled to touch the Bible, but you were very sick, very weak. I stopped reading, and beamed at you, convinced you were seeking to make contact with the Lord's words. But now I am remembering I cannot stop, and I am seeing what I chose not to see then. You were trying to shut me up. With what little strength you had left you were trying to make me stop. After smiling at you so that you must have felt skewered by my stupidity I kept reading. Cheerfully reading. You closed your eyes; I recall the lids were almost transparent and I could see the globes of your eyes through the papery skin, and I kept reading. How else were you to get away except to die? I hounded you to death.

I stumble out from behind the bushes, put my foot in the puddle. In bewilderment I stare at my spattered stockings. I raise my hand to tidy my hair, the familiar gesture of putting things in order an automatic comfort. Skin is hanging from the fleshy mound of my palm, as insubstantial as onion skin. Only the blood oozing from under the shredded flesh attests to life. The sky swings above my head, light beating relentlessly. I sway to the rhythm of the sky, my hand held out before me like a mascot, dripping blood. I've prayed to God for help all my life and now He reveals the mystery of His spiritual guidance. My world is rocking, my balance threatened, but He steadies me. I stay on my feet.

Mrs Maguire is galloping across the road. I haven't seen her run like that for years. And then she's in front of me, anxious face filling my frame of vision, emitting small noises of concern like a signal tower.

'It's all right dear. I'm just—' but I don't have a word for what is happening.

Mrs Maguire fusses me across the front lawn and down the driveway. Her clucking is annoying and soothing me both. Suddenly I am much too tired to resist and I let her lead me inside and bathe my shredded flesh.

'Do you have bandages?' she asks. I point her to the bathroom and sit on the chair she pulled into the centre of the kitchen to catch the light, nursing my wounded hand. 'I'm sorry James,' I say.

'What was that Mrs Grace?' Mrs Maguire peers at me with real concern as she hurries into the room, bandages and pins in her hands.

'I said I'm sorry dear,' I lie through my teeth, 'for putting you to all this trouble.' My reputation will really be down the gurgler if she thinks I'm talking to myself.

She bandages my hand. 'I'm not sure that you shouldn't take this to a doctor to be looked at.' She clucks at me again. 'Oh dear, oh dear, how did you do this?'

I'm feeling much better for having lied. I think perhaps I should have taken up lying much earlier in life. Without warning I am shaken with fury. Fury with my mother, whose provision for me knocked any sense clean out of my head, and fury with myself, for having succumbed so spinelessly.

My bandaged hand is a neat white stump. 'Shall I put the kettle on?' Mrs Maguire asks.

'Thank you. That would be lovely.' I admire my stump. 'You've done a very nice job.'

'Do you remember what happened?'

I realise I haven't answered her question yet. She's worried now that I'm suffering memory loss. I have done, I could confess, for most of my life, but not any more. Not any more.

But I resist the urge to tell her that I damaged my hand whilst remembering that I helped kill my brother. I think another lie is called for, just a little one.

'I tripped over myself and fell against the wall. Old skin, you know, it doesn't stand up to much.'

Mrs Maguire is relieved. I can see her thinking that I've not yet lost my marbles. 'I saw you standing there, reeling, and I just ran.'

'I got quite a shock when I saw what I'd done to my hand, and I couldn't think what to do. I do believe,' I say, giving her a winning smile, 'that you've saved me. It was very kind of you.'

She reddens and murmurs, busies herself with the kettle and teapot. I'm feeling very tired again. I'm not sure I can stay sitting up. I'm also not sure if I can manage any more winning smiles. Mrs Maguire turns to fetch teacups and notices. 'You're done in aren't you?' I nod, and she turns the gas off under the kettle. 'I'll take you in to lie down.'

I settle on my bed, hands crossed on my chest, the position of repose. Mrs Maguire tells me she'll check on me in the evening and leaves, the venetian blinds on the door rattling for a few seconds after she pulls it closed behind her. There is silence, spreading and pooling through the house, through me. From outside I can hear birds twittering in the crepe myrtles, the cries of children at play, the hum of red brick houses crosshatched in orderly fashion around me. I have always had an orderly life. And underneath, these disorderly feelings that have never been killed off. Not for want of trying. I tried. Mum tried. But not Bert. He looked at me and saw the chaos within and he was not afraid.

It's an odd feeling to find yourself all giggly and light-hearted at sixty. Other people look at you with dismay, as if being silly belongs to youth only. There I was, in my sensible shoes, my plain dresses (even my good frocks simple and unadorned, but in softer colours or fabrics, with a hat to match), my horn-rimmed glasses (that was the era, not me; everyone wore horn-rims, but it was a particularly severe look on me) in love. Bert would only have to phone or visit and I became skittish and fluttery. Even when he was not around I was different, visibly softer. Mum was frantic.

Bert joined our meeting following Margaret's death. He sold their house, finding it too big for just one, and the move led him to us. To me. He was welcomed at our fellowship, for his preaching skills and his genuine nature. My mother also made him welcome until it became clear that when he came over to speak with us at the close of the meeting he was coming to speak with me, not her. It took me some time to notice it myself, I was so unused to being sought out. When I did notice I turned aside my mother's suggestions that we not tarry, that we go home directly following the final prayer. The more she suggested, the greater became my determination to stay. Bert courted me in the most seemly fashion, in public, amongst our brethren, in front of my mother. I welcomed his courtship and there was nothing my mother could do to stop it.

For the past forty years I'd lived quietly at home, attending meetings, circulating tracts (Mrs Maguire was not the only person in the neighbourhood to feel the breath of my righteousness upon her), keeping house for Mum. James' death struck hard at Dad, and his health deteriorated again, leaving him as only a husk of himself. I didn't know what he and Mum spoke of in their privacy but I do know that Dad and I had little to say to each other. We had become polite strangers, boarding in the same house. One day in the garden, as I was weeding, I looked up to see Dad sitting shrivelled in a chair, soaking up the late sun, a rug over his knees, and remembered that this was the man who had placed me so tenderly in that blanket-lined wheelbarrow following my illness, so that I would enjoy the garden. I remembered that he had trickled earth through my palms and with that gesture had passed a love of gardening to me. Soil and passion had intermingled as he taught me how to feel the earth and osmotically the capacity to grow things had become mine. I looked at Dad and remembered these things and yet it was as if I were looking at another man. I was kneeling on rich black soil, my trowel plunged into the loamy stuff and I looked from the soil to Dad and tried to put the two together. There was no connection, not even enough to tell him what I was remembering.

Dad died when I was twenty-nine and then it was just Mum and me. We sold the house at Baulkham Hills and moved to a smaller one at Penshurst. I never enquired as to how we were supporting ourselves—Mum took care of all that. I know there was property, because each Saturday I would go with Mum to collect rent from the tenants. When she died she had nothing, except her house, yet beside the property she inherited when Dad died I'm sure she acquired more as time went on. She liked business, it suited her. I think she started selling the properties after I married Bert and I hazard that she donated the proceeds to the church. She never did approve of my marriage.

Forty years in the wilderness. It would be reassuring to say *like Christ*, but unfortunately, unlike the dear Lord, I was not thinking during that time. So it was forty years of foolishness, not spiritual growth. Yet something was simmering under the starch of faith, because when Bert appeared I discovered I was much more flexible than I'd thought.

It disturbed Mum to see me so pliant and distracted. It had been just the two of us for the last thirty years and we'd acquired habits of being so much alone with each other. Mum liked to read the Bible while I made the tea, she liked to hold onto my arm when we went out, she liked to remind me I had left it too long since cleaning the silver last, when invariably it was the next chore on my list. I liked to provide good wholesome meals for both of us, and keep our house neat and our clothes in good condition and, truth to tell, I liked occasionally to use my partial deafness as a convenient excuse when I chose not to hear some order from Mum. We were used to each other.

When Bert came along it changed everything. I wasn't used to him but wanted to be; Mum wasn't used to him and had no intention of becoming so, and he wasn't used to us and for the first time I saw Mum and I through an outsider's eyes and it was a shock. Mum and I were like an old married couple. This greatly disturbed me but there was Bert, a lifeline. And there was Mum, equally disturbed, but sinking.

I lift my bandaged hand to the light and study the folds of white crepe. I did become a nurse, after all, but not in public. Never in public, just at home. First Mum, then Bert. The question clangs around in my head. Now me? There isn't anyone to nurse me, and I'm not going into a home, as they so falsely call them. The neighbours are fine for a day wound, such as this, but I cannot look to them for that slow sinking that could overcome me. I lie my wounded paw on my chest and stare at the ceiling. Bert used to worry about me sleeping so still and unmoving. It's unnatural he'd say. People move in sleep. I wake up sometimes and worry that you're dead. I felt for him, but there are some habits impossible to break. This is a relatively small one. I changed the ones that mattered.

There's a commotion at the side of the house; a car engine loud outside the wall behind my head, the sound of voices, a car door closing. I think I hear Deborah's voice but she's not been to my house in a dozen years or more. I lie there wondering what I've got in the cake tin for visitors. Did I make a date loaf last week? I can't remember. I turn my head on the pillow to ease my discomfort. I'm not really up to visitors, I'm not sure how I'm going to get up to greet them.

Then I hear Kimberley's wail of protest and I know it is Deborah. She comes into the room, the baby's din filling up the space immediately. She seems concerned.

'Penshurst doesn't suit Kimberley,' I say. It's a stupid thing to say.

'She'd better get used to it,' Deborah answers. 'She can't stay in Paddington all her life. What sort of ideas would that give her?'

I hold up my thumb and forefinger, very close, only a thin gap between them. Deborah smiles awkwardly. 'Exactly.' Kimberley's racket is almost more than I can tolerate. It had been so peaceful lying here in my corpse's position and now here are Deborah and Kimberley, taking up so much room, clamouring loudly. I want them to go away. I close my eyes.

Deborah plumps herself down on the bed, wobbling the mattress, and I'm so surprised I open my eyes. 'Don't go to sleep on me Aunty, when I've come all this way to visit.'

Disbelief thumps in my chest. 'Don't think just because you choose to grace me with your presence that I have to entertain you.' The words shock me. I've not been that rude to anyone for a long time.

Deborah, however, smiles serenely. 'That's better. I thought for a moment you were going to go gently into the night.'

I'm still angry. 'If I do it's my own business.'

'No it's not. You've got family.'

'Family, family. I've done the right thing by my family all my life. Don't tell me about family.' Deborah transfers Kimberley to her other arm. Kimberley's face is red and mottled. I could hit her, anything to stop the noise. I sigh exaggeratedly. 'Deborah, take Kimberley away, there's a dear. I need to rest.'

'You think no one's going to notice if you just fade away?'

Rage helps me struggle to a sitting position. 'You'd be without a babysitter. That would be inconvenient now, wouldn't it?'

Deborah remains calm. 'I'd be without you.'

I've nothing to say to that. My ill temper punctures and I lean back against the bedhead. Kimberley hiccups and goes quiet and the room is strangely silent and I, strangely, am feeling better. Not as exhausted as I was. I squint at Deborah. 'I've never argued with anyone like I argue with you.'

'Except your mother.'

'Is that what I did?'

'Yes. You just took a long time between bouts.' Deborah puts Kimberley on the bed and she crawls across my legs first one way then the other until she finds a satisfying section of mattress, where she begins to bounce. Even sitting down she can get the springs moving.

Deborah says, 'Kimberley's a terrible name. It's like some bad TV show. I suppose it's too late to change to Sarah, or Emma.' It's not really a question.

'Kimberley's what you named her.'

Deborah looks at her daughter with rue. 'She's going to hate me for that name when she's older. I don't know what I was thinking of.'

'Better that she hate you for a name than for a lot of other things.'

'She'll hate me just for being her mother. I guess her name will give her true cause for grievance. She can always change it by deed poll when she's older and throw that in my face.' Kimberley grins at us, a gummy, toothless grin. 'The way I'm talking about it makes it sound like I named her carelessly, or with less than affection, but in truth I thought I was offering her something.'

It occurs to me that perhaps my mother really did love her friend Annie Vale, and that even though she no longer had contact with her, by giving me her name she kept the friendship alive in her heart. It occurs to me that I've often misread my mother, seeing love where there was only the desire to control, and malice where there was love. For a couple who spent sixty years together we were temperamentally unsuited.

'What are you doing here?' I ask. Breaking a habit of twelve years seems to call for some sort of explanation.

'Is that an existential question, in which case I think I need a few more years to answer, or is it the more mundane question of how did I know something had happened to you?' I lift my white stump to indicate the latter. 'Mrs Maguire telephoned me—she checked your phone list.' Deborah gets off the bed and looks down the hallway. 'Nothing's changed. Your house is just as I remember it.'

'I don't have an interior decorator.'

Deborah wanders around the room, looking at photographs on walls, picking up objects on my dresser. 'It's not a bad way to go, is it, this slanging off at each other?'

I recall the Townleys, forever 'slanging off' at each other, that constant jokey, dig-in-the-ribs banter a net which bound them together and kept them imprisoned. I was fascinated by the repartee, longed to be under the net, and had no idea when young how to participate. Now I know that it's not so hard to do, and that the Townleys liked me precisely because

I couldn't play-act. 'It can disguise truer, deeper feelings,' I say to Deborah.

'Well of course,' she answers, 'how else are we to get through life?' I'm not sure if she's serious.

'Where's Peter?' I ask, meaning which city, which state, which country?

'He's not around.'

She is no longer being flippant. 'Has something happened?' I ask cautiously.

'No, but he's never around is he?'

'Neither were you, until recently.'

'I suppose not. But with Kimbles, you, I've made an effort, changed things.'

'You think he hasn't?'

'I guess I never noticed before how little we see of each other.' She busies herself with a crystal flask, examining it closely. 'When you talk of Bert I know you miss him. It's been more than five years and you still miss him. I'm not sure that I miss Peter. I just know that he's not around.' She puts down the flask. 'You seemed to have this perfect union with Bert.'

'Not perfect, no.' I consider. 'He was my first friend in forty years, the first person in a very long time to like me just for who I am. And he was so much easier to live with than my mother. He didn't criticise me all the time.'

'But you were always together. You did everything together.'

'He was easy to be with. And I'd been so terribly lonely for so long, without even knowing it, that I was happy to spend all my time with him.'

'Peter and I do hardly anything together.'

'You made Kimberley together.' She gives me one of those looks young people give old people when they make some reference to sex. The sort of look that says, I didn't know you knew about that. I think they forget where they came from

154

and start to believe they sprang into being fully formed, dressed to go out. I think they imagine they invented sex.

But Deborah rallies. 'Please Aunty, that took us all of twenty minutes. That doesn't make a marriage.'

'What does?'

She comes and sits on the bed again. Kimberley reaches for her and Deborah pulls her daughter onto her lap. 'Do I like Peter? Do I know who he is? We haven't had a conversation for so long, a real one, like this, not one of those *will you pay the house insurance or will I?* ones, that I don't know that I know him.'

Kimberley, bored and restless, arches her spine and throws her body into the air. There is a sharp crack as her head hits Deborah's chin and then she's crying fit to bust, howling inconsolably. I see that Deborah's fighting back tears whilst she comforts Kimberley. Either it hurt like billyo or she's distressed by what she's been saying. Maybe both.

Deborah paces up and down the room, saying there there, over and over again, but Kimberley cannot be comforted. 'Aunty, I'm sorry, I'll take her outside.' They leave the room and Kimberley's sobs drift down the hall in receding bursts, the sound of a retreating army. Expecting devastation to flood in once more, I experience instead a great wash of calmness. I inspect my bandaged hand. Torn flesh is a small price to pay for dismantling the walls in my memory, walls that I had built to last a lifetime. I press my crepe-wrapped hand to my chest, to mark the rude discomfort that even the calmness cannot displace. Two lives were at stake and only one survived. Well, I barely survived. Like prisoners of war we were responsible for each other's wellbeing and I threw my lot in with the camp guards, thinking it would protect me. James threw himself against the electric fence instead. Now, like any survivor of torment, I'm left with my guilt. I'm not fully responsible, but I can no longer disclaim all responsibility. I can no longer forget.

I recall the legend Bert related when preaching. It had always left me uncomfortable and I'd persuaded myself it was because it was not a very good fable. I decided Bert was best as a preacher when he spoke directly from himself, that metaphors and analogies were not for him. In the story the Son of God was nailed to the Cross and died, He went straight to hell and set free all the sinners there in torment. And the Devil wept and wailed for he thought he would get no more sinners for hell. Then God said to him, 'Do not weep, for I shall send you all those who are self-righteous in their condemnation of sinners. And hell will fill up again till I return.'

I hear Bert's voice, and then I hear myself, a scratchy sound in the silence. It's my laughter I am hearing.

My hand heals slowly. Deborah and I agree that I should rest for a week, as I am not able to manage Kimberley with only one hand. I've been concerned for some time as to my ability to care for her for another year or two, and now I oscillate between believing that the week's rest will reinvigorate me and fearing that I have already passed the point of being capable of caring for an infant. I am grateful for the delay in having to face this, although I know it must be faced. I keep thinking, not yet, not yet.

What cannot be postponed is the appointment with the homeopath. However, I cannot drive and Maggie does not drive, so I decide we will go by taxi, even though Dr Cooper has his rooms at Chatswood, on the other side of Sydney, a good forty-five minutes away. Maggie is already nervous, and becomes more so with the realisation that she cannot pretend to be simply going to the shops with me. She's about to withdraw from the appointment, but I tell her not to fuss anymore, and to meet me at my front gate as agreed, that I'll hear no more of her bleating. Surprisingly, it works. Maggie goes quiet, and shows up the next morning dressed in her good clothes, meek as a lamb. I'm relieved to have no more bother, but I think I sounded very much like my mother and it disturbs me to note how submissive Maggie became under the direction of my mother's tone.

I chat in the taxi about nothing in particular, and Maggie occasionally responds, but by the time we get to Dr Cooper's she is silent with terror. I know it is terror, I recognise it too well. We sit in the waiting room, our hands patient in our laps. My hands are still. Maggie's hands tremble. When Dr Cooper calls I urge Maggie to go first; it would be inhuman to ask her to wait further.

She stands up and looks at me, slightly puzzled. 'Aren't you coming in?' she asks.

'I will if you want me to, but this is your time with the doctor. It might be best for you to go alone.'

She is momentarily undecided. Being offered privacy is not something she is used to. 'I'll go alone,' she says, giving me a quick sidelong look in case I've changed my mind.

'I'll be here,' I say.

She is gone a long time. Dr Cooper finally appears and asks me to join them. I know it is not good news, she's been a bad colour for too long. Entering the room I make a decision, although before that I had not known I was considering the issue. I decide that I will not offer nursing care, or even the sort of daily checking in that might be required. Of course I will call in, frequently, but I don't want the responsibility of being the major provider of care. The question, however, is not even put to me. Maggie is indeed very ill, but she sits calmly, agreeing to every suggestion Dr Cooper makes. She is a quite different woman to the ashen-faced one who waited with me not so long before. I realise that she is going to die, and that she is glad of it. I recognise that desire to get away, to be done with life, because I've seen it before in James. I attend to Dr Cooper, who is being kind and reasonable, neither denying all hope nor offering false hope, and I know that this is Maggie's choice and I have nothing to do with it. I need not help her die, as I did James, I need only bear witness.

In the taxi on the way home she takes my hand. It is such an unusual gesture for her that I am taken aback, but it goes unnoticed. She is in a state of beatitude. I understand it, but I do not approve. There are other choices, I want to insist, there have always been other choices. Death is such a cowardly solution.

'Thank you for taking me,' Maggie says. 'Everything will be all right now.'

'No dear,' I reply, 'everything will be difficult and painful.'

She is startled. I have cut across the dream of death. But she recovers and says, 'Everything will be all right, you'll see.'

Anger sours my mouth and I turn to look out the window. I see James' skeletal face staring up from the pillow, all pretence at fighting for life long gone, and I understand that I am not responsible for his death. I turn back to Maggie, cocooned in her blissful self-destruction, and the taste of my anger is the taste of life itself. It is the harder choice to not die.

At home, in the garden, I survey my terrain. Thy kingdom on earth, I think, savouring the familiar contours, paraphrasing a bit. Did Mrs Chapman ever come to know a kingdom on earth, I wonder? She never did get her melaleucas. 'Don't be a stranger,' she'd said to me, on that last visit, yet that is precisely what I became. Another thing that can't be changed.

I watch a sparrow wrestle with a worm foolhardy enough to surface, despite the heat of the day, like a car travelling up a ramp leading from the freeway, ignorant of the glaring signs proclaiming, *Wrong Way, Turn Back.* You have to worry about some of God's creatures at times, plainly going against their natures. That worm should know that at this hour he's supposed to be burrowing deeper into the earth, not away from it. But they say that's what helps us grow, helps us to evolve, to go against set patterns and trust to a different instinct. I can accept that, I'm not one of those people who can't fit evolution and God together.

Mum couldn't. When I evolved into a woman in love it was what could be termed a startling development. Mum's lips set into even grimmer lines as Bert came to visit more and more often and when we announced we were going to be married she couldn't even manage a congratulation. Well why should she? She didn't feel it. On our wedding day Bert and I were luminous with happiness and Mum evinced disapproval with every gesture. The photos of that day show Bert and I grinning like Cheshire cats on either side of Mum, who stands dour between us, her hat and her lip pulled down, giving her the look of a grumpy brownie.

Bert and I bought the house next-door to Mum's. We set a gate in the fence dividing the two properties and I continued to cook and clean for her, as well as for Bert and myself. We settled into a pattern, not so different from before, with Bert at the nursery during the day, Mum and I involved in household matters and the three of us attending meetings on the weekend.

It was at one of the meetings that a friend pulled me aside. Bert had preached that day and I was full of the goodness he always managed to impart with his words.

'I thought you should know,' my friend said, 'that your mother has been,' she searched for the word, 'talking.'

Her choice of word did not illuminate me. 'Talking of what?'

Constance's voice dipped lower. 'Talking about Bert.'

Some cold premonition gripped me. 'Talking in what way?'

Constance looked around quickly. In that instant I understood that other people were also afraid of my mother. I had never considered this possibility before. 'She's been hinting, well more than hinting, that he preaches one thing but does another. She's mentioned alcohol, and another woman.' I think the look on my face almost stopped her, but she gamely continued. 'They're talking about not letting him preach any more.' Our eyes met. 'I'm so sorry,' she whispered.

'Don't be,' I said.

I had never been close to Constance, although I called her a friend because we visited hospices together and spoke after meetings. So we were acquaintances really, and my choice of the word friend reveals how little I understood its meaning. I did not have a good track record with friends. Bert was the first person I had laid myself open to, and allowed myself to stay open to, and that was helped by the fact that he was my husband. The one element I'm proud of in the whole sorry mess that followed was that I did not turn from Constance, as I experienced the urge to do, but did, in fact, become friends with her. She was my first female friend since Marion Townley, and although I refused to allow myself to think about how shabbily I had treated Marion, I did not repeat history. It was difficult for me, because my training encouraged me to shut Constance out, especially as she had given me something, in this case information. It had not been easy for her, she was no gossip, but she had seen a terrible wrong developing, for she knew Bert to be a good man, and she had felt impelled to intervene. For me also it was not easy, but instead of shunning her I got to know her, and let her get to know me. She became my dear friend, and she saw me through Bert's slow dying, and Mum's. It was a great loss when she too died, only last year.

Bert drove us home after the meeting. I sat in front with him, Mum sat in the back. I turned to look at her and saw her head held high, saw a tiny stick of a woman lording it in the back seat of a Holden, acting as if she was above everything that surrounded her. I knew that look—hadn't I sat in the back of the carriage a lifetime ago manifesting equal disdain? You're not above anything, I wanted to tell her, except the wheels of a car.

When we arrived home I saw Mum into her house, as usual, while Bert put the car away. Normally Mum would take off her hat and gloves, change her frock and join Bert and me for Sunday dinner. Our two houses were as one, the gate in the fence a doorway between rooms.

I couldn't wait for Mum to change. I bailed her up in the hallway, put a restraining hand on her arm and turned her to face me. 'You had no right,' I said.

'What are you talking about?'

'You had no right to say those things about Bert. You're spreading lies to get back at me.'

Mum's face told me I was despicable. 'Go and get dinner Annie. You're becoming hysterical.'

Where I had no courage for myself I had courage for Bert's sake. 'You're a mean old woman. You've always been mean.'

Mum's voice was cold enough to skate on. 'You're raving. You think that if you insult me it will make you feel better for who you are. But you'll always be who you are—a stupid girl who has never found God.'

'God has nothing to do with this, except you're going to have some explaining to do when you get to heaven.'

Mum turned her back on me and started to walk away. I caught up with her and yanked at her arm. I yelled, 'Don't you walk away from me.'

Surprise flickered briefly. 'If we're talking about rights, you have no right to speak to me in this way.' She pointed, imperiously. 'Go and get dinner. Be a decent wife if you can't be a decent daughter. We will not speak of this further.'

For a moment I was that twenty-year-old girl, shovelling rage into sewn-up pockets on a glassed-in, green-tinged verandah. Yet as fast as I stuffed the stitches unravelled. I was that twenty-year-old girl and my sixty-one-year old self, and it was no longer a question of backing down. My anger was uncontainable.

'You have ruined my life. You have never wanted anything

good for me. I might be stupid but so are you. You're a stupid, mean old woman and you should never have attacked Bert.'

'Don't tell me I've ruined your life. You've done nothing with it—wasted God's gift to you.'

The familiar sense of having things upended, so that I no longer recognised them, was perilously hovering. I found myself literally brushing the sensation aside, like so many cobwebs, in order to see. My mother followed the movement of my hand. 'I have looked after you for most of my life. If you're telling me that was a waste of God's gift then I think I agree with you. That is not what God would have wanted for me.'

My even tone disconcerted Mum. 'If you're so sure what God wants for you what are you doing here?'

'I'm here to tell you that you are no longer welcome in my house.' I hadn't known I was going to say that and the words lay between us, a river widening with each passing second, the waters rising fast. From our separate banks Mum and I could see each other. I could hear the roaring of the flood in my ears and I expected that we would both go under.

'Don't tell me where I can and cannot go. I am your mother.'

Mum seemed to be shrinking as the river widened. The spread of water between us was changing the perspective. From where I stood she looked like a tiny old woman. 'You are my mother,' I said to this small bundle of bones, this little bird-woman, 'but you've gone too far. You are no longer welcome in my house.'

I saw the old woman gather herself. 'You are an ungrateful child,' she flung at me.

I considered her from the furthest shore. 'No,' I decided, 'I am not. That is not what I am.' I took a step back. 'I have to go and get dinner now. I will bring you yours when it's ready.'

'I don't want your food.'

'You don't have to eat it,' I said, reasonable, 'but if you

don't you're liable to starve to death. There's no one else to cook for you and I don't think you can do it for yourself anymore.'

The little bird-woman ruffled angry feathers and jabbed at me with her beak. 'My brethren will take care of me, especially when they find out what a monster I have for a child.'

'My brethren took care of me and look how I turned out.' That silenced her. 'I have to go and get dinner,' I repeated. 'I'll bring you yours.'

'You are making me a prisoner. I will complain to the authorities.'

'No one is a prisoner. There are no more prisons.' Mum stood shrunken in her clothes. For the first time in my life my big bones were a comfort to me. 'You're free to come and go as you please, but you're not free to come into my house. That's all there is to it.' I walked down the hall. At the back door I turned and said once more, 'That's all there is.'

I closed the door softly and walked along the path, through the gate and up the stairs to my back door. Bert was polishing his shoes in the back hallway, whistling tunelessly between his teeth.

'Hello there. Thought you'd got lost.' He must have seen disturbance in my face because his hands stilled, the brush poised in upward motion, the shoe jutting from his wrist like a question mark. 'Are you all right?' he asked.

'I think so,' I said. 'I'd better get dinner.'

I could feel him watching me as I went into the kitchen. I waited for the whistling to resume but it did not. I began to scrape the vegetables, thin strips of peel falling to the newspaper in reassuring colourful piles. My hands were a marvel to me, placing saucepans and baking dishes, unravelling the papery skin of garlic, gathering plates, topping and tailing beans in smooth and rapid motion. I was full of admiration for my hands, for their grace and sureness. I lifted them to the light, the better to see them. They were large and strong boned, but not fleshy, with the gold wedding band embellishing the column of my finger. Good strong capable hands, adroit and knowledgeable.

'And the Lord said, let there be light,' murmured Bert, who had come into the kitchen unbeknownst to me.

Slowly I brought my hands down from where they were stretched to the shafts of light angling through the window. More a gesture of celebration than supplication. 'And there was light,' I said, complementing Bert's quote.

He eyed me quizzically. 'Do you need a hand?'

'No,' I answered. 'I think I'm doing just fine on my own.' He nodded acquiescence. 'But it's nice to know you're there if I need you.'

He went outside and I opened the oven door and put the plates inside to warm. The rich odour of baked lamb, with an overlay of garlic and rosemary, pervaded the kitchen. The meat crackled and sizzled, almost done. I closed the oven door, amazed that our dinner had continued to cook whilst everything changed. Slowly roasting while we were at the meeting the lamb had surrendered its raw pink flesh to warmth and now was ready. Almost. There's nothing like a good slow roasting to transform base ingredients. That's the whole art of cooking. That's the theory behind hell too, only those poor souls are never pronounced done. Maybe that's the whole point of hell, that at a certain moment, instead of waiting for the heavenly chef to pronounce you ready, you take yourself out of the fire, knowing that if you stay any longer you'll dry up and be of no use to anyone, not even a carnivore with a taste for very well done meat? Maybe that's God's test, to see if you have the courage and trust to get yourself off the spit, with its certainty of endless fiery revolutions in a fixed rhythm, into a place shaped by the cool climate of doubt? Maybe no one is ever invited into heaven but people take themselves there, to risk living under the gaze of God? Goodness knows, He can't keep an eye on you in hell, but away from the fire everything is exposed. A slow roasting is no picnic but after you adjust to the heat and the dehydration the predictability becomes comforting. The more you cook the less you notice it. But out in the open, in a changing climate, certainty becomes a foreign language, imperfectly understood, making sense in snatches only.

Bert came into the room once more. 'Do you want me to carve?'

I slid the roast out of the oven onto the spiked carving platter. The potatoes and pumpkin, golden and encrusted, went back into the oven. 'God's a wily old fox,' I commented.

Bert was sharpening the carving knife, the metallic sound the song of the kitchen. 'I thought He was a shepherd.'

I pondered this. 'He is a shepherd. But He's also the fox who sends us bleating, seeking shelter.'

'Isn't that the Devil?'

Suddenly shaken with laughter I said, 'Or my mother.'

Bert gave me such a look I clutched my belly to hold in my laughing. He set up the knife music again, his hands held out before him, conducting the great roast choir. 'Or your mother,' he agreed.

And then we were both laughing fit to bust, while the vegetables browned and the roast quietly steamed.

I take tomatoes, cucumber and lettuce from my garden to Mrs Maguire to thank her for her care. A momentary mistrust sweeps her expression when she opens the door, but when she sees that it is vegetables I am holding, not tracts, she invites me in.

But I don't want to enter the house. I proffer my gifts, my thanks, and notice with some shock the age spots on the back of Mrs Maguire's hands. She is middle aged, although I have some notion of her still as being the young wife and mother who first moved in across the street from me. That was thirty-five years ago. I look at the soft folds of flesh of her face and neck and understand that she is now the age I was when I married. Her children have long since moved away.

'I miss the children,' I say. She looks startled, and I explain. 'There were always children playing in this street. Now we're all getting old.'

'It's true. The only kids are the Evans twins,' she points to a house at the far end of the street, 'and little brats they are too.'

We contemplate our street. 'I suppose we need people like me to die off so that fresh blood can move in,' I say.

'Mrs Grace!' She is clearly shocked.

'Don't worry, I have no intention of popping off yet. It was just a comment.'

Mrs Maguire leans forward confidentially. 'Frank and I are considering selling, and buying one of those villas.'

Images of the Mediterranean crowd my mind. 'Villas?' I murmur, somewhere between a question and assent.

'You know, those villas that are part of a whole complex. Part of a retirement village.'

Now it's my turn to be startled. 'You're hardly ready for one of those.'

'They're not nursing homes,' she says, reading my concern. 'The villages have all these different sorts of housing, one or two bedrooms, with or without garden, completely self-contained or fully serviced. But they're much smaller than this.' She flaps a hand at her house. 'Frank and I are tired of looking after all this. It's getting to be too much for the two of us.'

'I know *that* feeling. It's beginning to wear me down but there's nowhere else I'd rather be.'

'You could try a retirement village.'

I try not to look suspicious. 'At my age they'd assume I needed a nursing home.'

Mrs Maguire shakes her head. 'It's up to you to specify

what you want. They have to agree with you, of course, before they sign contracts, but it's clear to anybody that you can look after yourself.'

I say goodbye and wander back across the street. I *can* look after myself, although it's taken almost an entire lifetime for me to know it. And just at the very moment that I understand my own capability I realise I would like to step down from my high table of self-sufficiency and have others involved in the process of looking after me. Not as my mother did, through domination and force, defining me before I had the chance to shape myself, but in partnership, respectfully. That's how Bert approached me and why I loved him so.

Laughing like loons together about my mother strengthened my resolve but it wasn't easy. I took a plate of food, loosely covered by foil, into Mum. She wouldn't open the door to me so I left it on the doorstep. Bert and I chewed our way through our meal in silence. Mum's absence was an uncomfortable presence at the table and if someone had told me Mum had X-ray vision and was watching us through the walls I would have believed it.

We both pottered in the garden after lunch, the brooding frame of Mum's house constantly catching my peripheral vision. I'd not yet explained to Bert what I had done. I could not fully explain it to myself. I was deeply grateful for his companionship in the spring sunshine, his immersion in his own activities and his willingness to let me be, to not ask questions, but leave me the freedom to find out for myself what it was exactly that I was doing. Towards evening I glanced skywards to see a line of pigeons strung out against the hazed expanse of light like washing on a line. I couldn't see the beat of their wings but watched the line move across the sky as if pulled on a string. Bert was bent over a spade at the end of the garden bed, fully occupied. A rush of relief pumped through my bloodstream. Mum had always been so immersed in me and what I was doing. Every connection of thought and action, every move from intention to actuality had taken place under her gaze. I had thought it was God's gaze I was living under. At that moment, under a pearly sky, I felt that He'd been lucky to get a look in.

I prepared a light supper and again took a plate in to Mum. The house was furled tight against me. I didn't knock more than once; I had no desire to be a mendicant. Again I left the plate on the doorstep. The plate from lunch was still there, untouched, the meat and vegetables congealed and gummed under the foil.

Mum had no food in the house, at least none to sustain her, only a packet of tea, some milk and bran. She either had to leave the house, accept food from me or die. When I woke on Monday morning that last thought pressed on me, sat on my chest with urgency so that it hurt to breathe. She was angry enough to do it, to just sit there in her tomb of a house and starve to death, in order to punish me for my disobedience. Bert was still sleeping, his nose angled to the ceiling, his mouth ajar. In one slow sure movement—oh, I was still capable then of slow sure movements—I eased myself from under the covers and stood up. In the mirror I saw myself, a woman sliding past middle age to something older, my nightgown scalloping my ankles, my hands useless by my side, my face anxious and confused. I wanted to hammer Bert awake, to have him comfort me, but these were my demons to contend with. This was a familiar feeling, knowing that my mother would cause damage, even to herself, before she would loose me from her grip. I went to the bathroom and threw up and the foul smell and taste were a strange consolation. It wasn't pleasant to stand my ground.

I took a loaf of bread from the freezer, a half pound of butter and two eggs from the fridge, and a jar of jam from the cupboard and walked to Mum's door. The supper plate sat as I had left it. I walked round to the front door and let myself in with my key. The house was still and shaded, the ticking of Mum's grandfather clock in the hallway the only sound. I wanted to go forward on tiptoe, but I made myself walk as normally as I could, down the hall, past the empty bedroom, the silent lounge room, to the kitchen where Mum sat, fully dressed, hands firmly clasped in lap, back straight. You could have taken an architectural sounding for a wall true and sound from the line of her back.

We looked at each other for a long time, plumbing the silence. I did not feel the need to bridge it with words and it was Mum who eventually spoke first.

'Get out of my house,' she said.

The banality of her words was so unexpected that I laughed. I had thought Mum would have riven the silence with words of fire, but instead there was this, an entirely predictable response. Mum went very red in the face and shrieked, 'Get out of my house I tell you.'

'I've brought you some breakfast,' I said.

She came at me then, hands and nails aiming to punish me. She was a passionate little bantam rooster but my strength was greater than hers. I guess that's what comes of giving birth to a big-boned daughter. The jam jar and eggs broke on the floor and our struggle scrunched across the glass and gelatinous mess until I pinned Mum to her chair. We were both breathing hard, and for the first time Mum looked at me with the sort of look I imagine I'd had on my face when dealing with her all my life. I didn't feel victorious, just tremendously sad, and desperate to get back home to Bert.

I took my hands from her shoulders. 'Nothing's going to change Mum,' I reassured us both. 'I'll still do for you, and you're not a prisoner. Only you can't come into my house.'

Mum said nothing. It wasn't the end of it but it did feel like the beginning of something else. What I didn't say, but needed to, was that I hated her. I couldn't let myself fully know how I felt, although I know it now.

Torn flesh, I think, regarding the scars of my recent hand wound, is nothing.

'Miss Grace.' The words float down the hallway, small tangles of sound on air drifting towards me. The tendrils wisp around my face and swirl past me. 'Miss Grace,' I hear again, only this time the sound pushes at me like pellets. I feel the sharp sting on my face.

Marla stands before me. 'You deaf now Miss Grace?' she bellows, obviously put out. I am standing in the kitchen, looking out at the courtyard, Kimberley in my arms.

'No need to shout,' I say calmly. 'I can hear you perfectly well.'

'You wouldn't know it,' she says.

I am sick to death of being called, voices asking for me, searching out my whereabouts, intent on invading my solitary cogitation. But then I see myself, smugly aloof, refusing to acknowledge Marla, who has had to come tramping down the stairs to find me. I look at her work-reddened hands and thickened ankles and am ashamed.

'You senile now Miss Grace?' Marla asks suddenly. I'm not sure if her irritation has flexed to concern or if she is being mischievous.

How would I know if I was? It is so preposterous that I laugh out loud. 'No,' I say, while Marla scowls at me, her annoyance returned. 'I'm just being rude.'

'Oh la,' says Marla, hand on hip.

Now truly contrite I apologise. 'You're not the person to be rude to,' I acknowledge. 'That person died a long time ago.'

Marla perks up. This has interesting possibilities. 'Husband?' she asks.

'Mother,' I reply.

She nods sagely, hand still on hip, then jabs at me with her forefinger. 'I no your mother,' she says. 'You answer me next time.' I nod meekly. 'Good,' Marla says, satisfied that justice has been done. 'You hold that story about your mother. It good for afternoon tea. Now I go shopping.'

After she leaves I sit on my chair in the living room, watching Kimberley fight sleep. She sinks, then just at the point of depthless slumber, wrenches herself back to consciousness. Her eyeballs dance in their sockets with the strain. Again and again I watch her eyelids close and open, close and open until the weight of sleep keeps them shut, then see her violently wrestle herself awake. It must be exhausting. I wonder what it is that makes her so afraid to surrender to unconsciousness? Is she worried about missing out on something if she sleeps? What is there for her to see but the ceiling and the decorations on the cot and me sitting like a statue carved from weathered material?

The stubborness of us. Even here, at six months of age, the indomitable will. God must sleep deeply when He rests at night, having spent each and every day mustering His strength against our obstinacy. He's had His work cut out with me, not to mention my mother. Hold that story for afternoon tea, says Marla. How can I explain to her that there's not enough tea in China to see us through that story? Nonetheless, I hold it for her.

'So,' says Marla, settling back in her chair, inhaling the steam rising from her cup, 'you good daughter or bad daughter?'

I pause for a moment. 'Both.'

'Best that way,' she says. 'Me, I've always been good, but no matter, I'm still bad.'

This strikes me as such an essential truth that I have to balance my teacup carefully. 'Why so?' I ask.

'Husband no good, son no good. Me, I'm bad wife and mother.'

'Who says?' I ask, indignant.

'My mother.'

The injustice of it hurts. 'You support your family, you pay to bring them out here and your mother says you're a failure?' Marla nods. 'She thinks you're responsible for your husband and son?'

She nods again. 'My job to make sure everything OK. Everything not OK.'

'What do you tell your daughter?' I ask cannily.

'I tell her to make a good marriage and to make sure everything OK for her husband.'

I sit back, shocked. 'Marla, how can you, when you know it's unfair?'

Mischief crinkles her eyes. 'That when my mother in room. When my mother no in room I tell her be happy.'

I sit for a while, thinking. 'I was always good, but still a bad daughter, just like you. But then one day I was bad and it felt good.'

Marla rubs her ankle, where the flesh puffs over her shoe. 'Bet you took your mother by surprise.'

'Yes, I ambushed her and nothing was ever the same afterwards.'

'What you do?' I think she might start taking notes, she is so interested.

'I barred her from my house. She lived next door, so I went in every day to cook and clean, but she was not allowed to come into my house.'

I see that I have impressed Marla. 'And you want to be rude too. My, my.'

I put down my teacup. 'It was the best thing I ever did.' This, now, is absolutely clear to me. 'I have no regrets.'

Marla chews her lip. 'My mother live with me. Can't keep her in her room till she die.' I maintain a sympathetic silence. 'How long you keep your mother out?'

'Fifteen years.'

'Phew. You strong woman.'

'I was a desperate woman.'

Marla looks at me carefully. 'What happen next?'

'My mother died. I nursed her for the last year of her life, so that she could stay at home and not have to go into hospital.' I see Mum's head on the pillow, the early morning light dusting her thin hair, the scalp visible, transparent as bone china, her skin loose and dry and insubstantial as a cicada shell. She was beyond speech, and down to five and a half stone, a mere wisp of life, most of it in her eyes. Those eyes. They followed me everywhere, anchored me to her. Whenever I left the room I felt Mum's eyes on me still, refusing to acknowledge the imperatives of walls. I felt harried under those eyes, the criticisms that could no longer be voiced needling their way into existence with that jabbing gaze, pinning me to Mum's contempt.

Marla is saying something but I've been drifting. She waits patiently for me to refocus and repeats, 'So, you good daughter after all.'

Even as she speaks I experience a realignment of memory, so that Mum's eyes are no longer weapons but entreaties, offers of kinship. I think she had repented, and only her eyes could tell me. They were imploring, not attacking, seeking me out, not to hurt me but to ask forgiveness and heal the rift. As she lay dying my mother wanted something from me that she could not take but only humbly ask for. My forgiveness had to be freely given. It was not hers by right and she knew it.

Kimberley wakes up and begins to cry fitfully. Marla crosses the room and fiddles with Kimberley's nappy and the familiar stench fills my nostrils. Marla motions to me to keep my seat and ambles into the next room for a clean nappy, Kimberley against her chest, the crying soothed by touch.

So you good daughter after all, said Marla. She's right. I was. And at the end Mum knew it. My heart, good muscle that it

173

is, pumps full of blood, pumps fuller. I can hear my blood singing. All my life Mum looked at me, wanting a perfect daughter, something like a magnolia (*Beautiful*, everyone would say, *so like you*) or a jacaranda (*Splendid*, everyone would murmur, *what a wonderful presence*) or a maple (*A tribute to the home*), but instead she got me, a scrubby melaleuca. And only at the end of her life did she notice that I too had a dusting of blooms, small and delicate and designed for contemplation rather than show; that I was sturdy and enduring with my shape bent to the fortunes of circumstance; and that I was native to her garden. Not a transplant, but home-grown. Her very own bracelet honeymyrtle. It took her a lifetime to work out what was essential to her garden and what was not. Mum never was a gardener.

Deborah arrives home later than usual, full of apologies. I pour a Scotch for her, just how she likes it, and when I pass it to her she stops, right in the middle of something that she's rabbiting on about, her mouth a little circle of surprise. Her fingers close over mine as she takes the heavy-bottomed glass and she smiles, then she's off again, full speed to the dozen. I know she's fired up after work, but honestly, sometimes I think that girl should have been an auctioneer. She can rattle it off with the best of them.

In the morning I wake, the heavy clamp on my chest eased, miraculously it would seem, overnight. But I'm warier of miracles than I used to be. All that water into wine, all those restored limbs and Lazarus rising from the dead. Sheer hard work on the part of the Son of God, that's what it was. I'm sure that each time He never knew before He tried whether He could do it.

After breakfast I go into the garden. A honeyeater sips at the grevillea planted where the gate used to be. Its wings blur as it hovers, the movement silent from where I stand, no disturbance to the early morning peace. At the foot of the ramp a line of ants blockades the path, industrious and earnest. They're serious creatures, ants, not given to pranks or charmingly addled behaviour. I'm a bit of an ant myself.

There is a promise of heat but at present the air is mild and clean. I fetch my trowel from the outside windowsill of the laundry and head for the far end of the central garden bed. A thin film of moisture coats leaf and grass and I kneel to my devotions of soil and plant. The pumpkin vine rustles and I catch the whisk of tail as a cat jumps to the top of the fence, screened by the grapefruit tree. I think it is the grey from down the street. Bert would be pleased to know we have cats again.

I lurch to my feet, feeling the stiffness in my leg. I shuffle forward, my leg fumbling for its step, the length of thigh and calf a dead weight unwilling to work. Off-balance I take another step and then I'm falling, crashing, the concrete path rising with sickening speed toward me. I put out a hand to shield my face and try to turn my body, ungainly missile that it is, to land on the grass. There is a jarring of bone on cement, a thudding of me on stony matter. For a moment I feel nothing, know nothing, the sky a brazen blue lacerating my eyes. Like some giant anthill I lie there and then a terrible nausea spreads through me, the awful knowledge of my fall. The garden is very quiet, hushed with the fear jumbling inside me. I have already fallen but it is as if I am about to fall, the moment of the drop endlessly alive. I don't want to fall, I want to stop it, but I have already fallen. I am very frightened.

Seconds pass, maybe minutes, and I hear that I am whimpering. It is the only sound in the deathly quiet garden. I raise my head and look to the house. I am about half way down the yard, and the house seems a very long way away. I know I have broken bones, although I'm not sure which ones. I go to put my weight on my hands to raise myself and the astonishing pain in my right wrist leaves me gasping on the ground again. Agonisingly, as if I was a tortoise, I lift my head and look at my hand. It is broken at the wrist, unfamiliar in its odd angle. I have fallen on my right side and feel bruised and shocked down the length of my body. Leaning on my elbow I try to move and excruciating pain in my pelvis nails me once more to the concrete. I hear myself moaning. Tears rush to my eyes. The worst has happened, I know the worst has happened. I have broken my hip.

I go to call out but only a feeble noise escapes me. I lie there, fighting back the panic, and then I find my voice. 'Maggie,' I call. 'Maggie. Help.'

I hear my voice, a fragmented sound of alarm, but there is no answer. Nothing stirs on the other side of the fence. I call again for my neighbour but she does not answer. I am alone.

I have lost my bearings. I do not know how long I have lain here, with no one to notice that I have fallen. Dried saliva encrusts the corners of my mouth. I stare into the pitiless eye of the sky and then I see that He is watching me. He knows I've come a cropper. I am not alone.

I grit my teeth and roll onto my belly. I am shot through with pain, it is all I know. Whimpering loudly I roll over onto my left hip and elbow, my right elbow angled from my body to act as ballast, its useless hand a flag at half-mast. I inch my way down the path, my right leg dragging, the smashed hip protesting. Sweat smears my face, clots my vision. I can hear the grinding of my teeth. I cannot do this. The pain is too much. I will not make it to the house. I slide my left elbow along the ground, feeling the concrete abrade the skin, and progress another inch. Help me, I hear, not knowing if I have spoken out loud or cried only to myself. I feel God's hand on my back and I continue. I do what I cannot possibly do. I reach the foot of the ramp and fall into blackness.

Consciousness punches me. The pain is all that exists. I am at the foot of the ramp, looking up to the back door. I thank

God for having left the ramp in. I could not have managed stairs. I crawl up the ramp and lift my right arm to the latch. I bash the useless hand against the handle, sending currents of anguish through my arm, so that for a moment I think I will black out again. But I hold onto consciousness and the door is ajar. With my right elbow I push it fully open and recommence my slow progress of torment across the lino of the back hallway and kitchen. The house is cool and familiar and I start to cry, but I do not rest. I reach the carpet in the living room and snail my way across its endless expanse. I stop at the phone table, my breath coming in ragged tearing bursts. Dear Lord, I cry aloud. God! God! I reach for the phone cord and pull and keep pulling until the phone crashes off the table onto the floor next to my head. I could have hit myself. I dial 000 and request an ambulance. They hear whatever there is to hear in my voice and tell me one is on its way. I surrender to the blackness.

Swimming to the surface I am irritated by a persistent ugly noise. Stop, I say, or think I say, but the rataplan continues. I turn my head and see that the phone is off the hook. I fumble for the receiver and replace it and sweet peace descends upon the house. Upon me. I lie on the carpet, my fractured body the word of God, telling me what I have known for some time but have not been able to face, that I can no longer care for myself. There will be no more Kimberley, no more ferrying myself back and forth to Paddington, no more maintaining a large house and garden. For an instant fear floods me and the pain rises with the tide of terror. What if I die? The hip needs operating on. What if I do not surface from the anaesthetic? But it is change I am frightened of. The realisation calms me and I shift my back, trying to ease the pain, trying to get comfortable. The pain cannot be eased.

The pain is constant but the fear is tidal. It has receded, left me standing on an empty beach, ringed by monumental cliffs, the air so fresh and salty it tastes like ambrosia. Only my footprints mark the sand, the path I have taken glitters in the sharp light. I look back and see how far I have come, how exposed I am in the middle of this splendid beach, this trackless sand. I lift my head, raise my arms to the illimitable sky. Everything shines, polished and burnished with light, buffed to radiant perfection. My heart swells, is full, fuller still. I stretch out my arms, embracing the radiance. Nearer my God to Thee.

SCRAPING THROUGH STONE

JUDITH FOX

Sibylla, born into a family of wealth in England in the time of Richard Coeur-de-Lion, flees her home on the eve of her arranged marriage. She cuts her hair short, disguises herself as a boy and resolves to join Richard's Crusades.

Dominic is the only son of the unhappy union of a Scots lord and his French wife. Shame stains his family and Dominic looks to the Crusades to restore honour to his household. He becomes a Knight of the Order of St John of Jerusalem, pledged to obedience, chastity, poverty and the defence of Jerusalem.

In a fortress in Syria Dominic lives a life of steel and stone, embracing order. But Sibylla knows already that disorder governs life. As they search for individual freedom, they unexpectedly find each other.

Set amidst the dust haze of the Holy Land, drenched in the blood and savagery of the Crusades, *Scraping through Stone* is an exquisitely crafted fable about the mysteries of love and faith. Exploring the nature of self and identity in the face of loss, grief and chaos, it is a triumphant celebration of love.

ISBN 1 86508 712 2

THE CITY OF SEALIONS

EVA SALLIS

'A rich book—a lyrical account of a girl's growth and self-discovery, and at the same time a deeply sympathetic exploration of Muslim culture.'

—J.M. Coetzee

A luminous book about language, identity, culture and family; about a refugee mother who lost them all and a daughter who went to find them.

Lian is a stranger in a strange land, fighting her mother, Phi-Van, from afar. Haunted by her mother's story, Lian has run to the other side of the world, only to discover the true nature of what it means to be an outsider. As she loses herself in the confusing life of Yemen, her new foster mother country, she cannot see that the tyranny of Phi-Van's greater suffering is also her lifeline. But she must break too before she can grow.

This is a rich and strange journey under the sea to the place that defines and limits us all.

ISBN 1 86508 617 7

FINDING ULLAGUNDAHI ISLAND

FABIENNE BAYET-CHARLTON

Creating new boundaries of fiction and memoir, Fabienne Bayet-Charlton's strong and original voice carries us with her in *Finding Ullagundahi Island*.

'Softly, quietly so as not to wake old feelings, and maybe old spirits, Nana speaks about her life, about her family, her childhood, before the desert. She talks of her home, the strength of her childhood. She tells me about a river so wide, blue and meandering that her people lived in the middle of it, and trees so dense in numbers, so thick with leaves, they created a canopy of green mist throughout the land.

I sit there with my feet planted in acrid red dust, looking into my pale tea. Not believing ...

"How can people live on a river, Nana? Like it's land? How can a river be that big?"

Nana eyes me up and down, like a wise old turtle.

"Because it is." She sighs, sips her tea and says nothing more.'

This fresh, lively memoir about family, place and a sense of belonging, identity and Aboriginality draws you in and holds you. Fabienne has a voice of honey when writing about landscape and Dreaming stories and she tells acutely and lovingly about family, childhood and memories.

1 86508 586 3

THE BLACK BUTTERFLY

KATHLEEN STEWART

A decade ago, Julia Callaghan, now 29 years old, knew what it was like to be a movie star. Plucked from drama school and critically acclaimed in her first film, an incredible acting career seemed a certainty. But somehow it never happened. Her most successful role since has been her almost impervious self-delusion.

And then Patrick, athletic, handsome and chronically dishonest, comes into her life. A one-night stand that enthrals Julia unfortunately doesn't have the same effect on him. And Patrick's finding it difficult to cope with the consequences.

This acerbic, witty novel puts these two self-obsessed people together in the narcissistic 1980s, and surrounds them with mirrors of the traps they've unwittingly set for themselves.

Stewart's writing belongs in a category all of its own. With a wickedly humorous style, she constricts the lens of her characters' vision and chronicles their chaotic lives.

1 86508 560 X